The desire in her chilled and died

Tara had yielded to his seductive kisses, but at the sound of approaching footsteps outside her window, she struggled to be free of Dracon's imprisoning arms.

"Someone is coming! Don't—" she begged.

"Yes," Dracon said. "Charlot. As in any well-planned coup, the timing is all—" And bending to her again he took her lips with the same mastery as before.

As the footsteps stopped, then moved on, running, Tara realized it had all been a performance for Charlot's benefit.

"You meant Charlot to see us, as if—"

"As if we were lovers. I in your room; you—" Dracon's glance raked her flimsy negligee "—prepared for me."

JANE ARBOR
is also the author of these
Harlequin Romances

Many of these titles are available at your local bookseller.

For a free catalogue listing all available Harlequin Romances
and Harlequin Presents, send your name and address to:

HARLEQUIN READER SERVICE
M.P.O. Box 707, Niagara Falls, NY 14302
Canadian address: Stratford, Ontario N5A 6W2

Where the Wolf Leads

by

JANE ARBOR

Harlequin Books

TORONTO • LONDON • LOS ANGELES • AMSTERDAM
SYDNEY • HAMBURG • PARIS • STOCKHOLM • ATHENS • TOKYO

Original hardcover edition published in 1980
by Mills & Boon Limited

ISBN 0-373-02396-0

Harlequin edition published April 1981

CHAPTER ONE

MALE eyes followed Tara Dryden's slim figure as she walked the length of the hotel's inner foyer towards the open doors of the dining-room.

For an evening date she usually piled her russet hair high, a severity of style which emphasised the long column of her neck and throat. Seen from the side tables which dotted the foyer, her clear-cut profile was arresting, and her long-sleeved dinner dress of silver-grey silk jersey with its slashed skirt was a contrast in modesty and allure. The gown was new; she had dressed in carefree anticipation of a pleasant evening and she knew she was looking her best.

She was making for a corner near a bank of flowers where, on the other occasions they had met, the young Frenchman, Charlot Leloupblanc, had been awaiting her, ready to order her choice in aperitifs before they had gone into the dining-room or taken a taxi to a different restaurant. But tonight he was not there, and as she hesitated an usher approached her.

'Miss Dryden? Monsieur Leloupblanc's guest?' he questioned, and at her nod, led the way straight into the dining-room to a table from which, at sight of them, a man rose and stood—a man who was not Charlot.

5

This man was older—in his late thirties, Tara judged—and was urbane in a formal dinner-suit, where Charlot favoured the latest thing in velvet and frilled shirting. He was dark, with hair swept back and shaped to his nape; there were flecks of gold in his deep-set eyes hooded by heavy lids; his mouth was a cryptic, slightly disdainful curve; his tall figure was lean and hard-set, in contrast with Charlot's narrow-hipped grace.

'Thank you.' A flicked finger and thumb dismissed the usher, and the stranger addressed Tara, 'Miss Tara Dryden? You were to meet my cousin Charlot here, I think?'

Half enlightened, Tara said, 'Yes, I was expecting to. We had a date. But you are——?'

'Dracon Leloupblanc. Charlot will have mentioned me?' It was no question but so assured an assumption that he had been described to her that she longed to reply with a bland denial of having heard of him.

But of course she had. During their swiftly ripening friendship Charlot had been expansive on the subject of his family, an unusual grouping of people at his château home in the Gironde region of France.

The current bachelor head of the family was Dracon, a shipper of château-bottled Bordeaux wines, serving the many vineyards of the area, though not a grower himself. Sharing the house were Charlot and his mother, the widow of Dracon's uncle, Henri Leloupblanc, and Elaine Dorsay, a girl of eighteen to whom Henri had been guardian until his death, and who, five years Charlot's junior, had grown up with him. Henri Leloupblanc, with far less business acumen than Dracon's now dead father, had never been much more than a dependant upon the firm, and Dracon, the heir to it, had taken on the unwritten guardianship of Elaine and the support of his aunt when Henri had died. When Charlot had done his military service, he had gone into the Château d'Isray firm as a reluctant trainee salesman—and hated his job still, he had told Tara.

'But when Dracon says No or Yes, that becomes the law. Even before he was thirty he was running everything. *Le Loup Blanc*—the fabulous white wolf! You'd think Dracon had invented the name himself, *for* himself as the family leader, and though we are Leloupblancs as much as he is, I remember that even my father was half afraid of him, and he certainly has my mother and me by the nose. Elaine too, when she steps out of line,' he had grumbled.

'Does she—Elaine Dorsay—have a job?' Tara had asked.

'No. She lives at home, a companion for my mother.'

'But you—if you're repressed there and don't like your work—why don't you leave and do something else?'

At which Charlot had thrown her his charming ingenuous smile which she had begun to find melting to any differences between them.

'Perhaps because, in my heart, I'm a *little* afraid of cousin Dracon myself. Or because I have no real career and not much money of my own, and I do rather enjoy the fleshpots provided by Dracon at Isray, and shall want them for my wife if I marry,' he had admitted, adding the correction, '*When* I marry——' with a meaning under-the-lashes glance at Tara which she had understood.

At the time she had accused him of exaggerating Dracon Leloupblanc's tyrannical hold upon his relatives. Yet tonight, when the alleged monster murmured, 'You will dine with me'—making an order of it, rather than a request, for some reason equally compliant as they, she found herself obeying, as she took the chair he had drawn out for her from the table.

She told herself she should have demanded from him Charlot's whereabouts, and on being told—for he must know them!—have left him, her dignity safe. Instead she found herself committed to the bizarre obligation to him for a meal, never having met him before.

He laid aside the menu-card the table waiter had handed to him. He said, 'I see from your expression I needn't add to whatever you have heard about me from Charlot. He will have been graphic, I am sure, and I won't embarrass you by asking you to repeat it. But naturally you will want to know why he is not here to meet you, and I am?'

Tara bowed her head slightly. 'Naturally,' she confirmed. His English was as fluent as Charlot's, but where to Charlot she might have replied, 'Go ahead,' an echo of his cousin's formality seemed more in place.

(How hypnotised by a man's manner could one get?)

He said, 'Of course. And so I have sent Charlot home.'

Equally he could have sent a five-year-old to bed! Tara stared at him, open-mouthed. 'You have *sent* him home?' she exclaimed, to the acute interest of a couple at a nearby table. 'Home? To France? To—to——?' The picture of debonair, handsome Charlot being turned in his tracks and sent packing was too much, and she broke off.

Imperturbably his cousin agreed, 'That's so. Back to Isray. My reason? Because he had well overstayed his business time in London. Though——' a pause as Dracon leaned back and allowed his heavy-lidded eyes to rake her figure meaningly—'one need scarcely wonder why he lingered so long. You grace your profession charmingly, Miss Dryden, if I may say so. And I may?'

'Thank you.' There was irony in Tara's acknowledgement of the suave compliment. But if the sarcasm got through to him he ignored it and went on,

'However, he was supposed to be on a business trip, and I had to call a halt to his dalliance by coming over myself and sending him back. A disappointment for you, I realise; even a professional loss. Which latter I shall hope to make good to you——' He reached across to open her menu-card for her and opened his own. 'Shall we choose now?' he enquired, obviously oblivious of how, listening to him, her wits had gone whirling in search of reality and had found none.

'A grace to your profession.' The missing of an evening date 'a professional loss'. What *could* the man mean? Did he think——? But suddenly the kaleidoscope shivered into shape. That *was* what he thought— that she was a high-class call-girl, and Charlot had been the innocent prey which he had snatched from her predatory claws! Charlot Leloupblanc, a man of twenty-three, vouched for and recommended by a V.I.P. compatriot to the exclusive escort bureau where Tara had been working as a temporary secretary——! Charlot, victim of a vice organisation! Oh——! That was the long exhalation of breath with which she weathered the shock.

The next few minutes were a blur. Reluctant to consume food which would be paid for by this odious man, she ordered the least she could—a consommé and a veal escalope—while debating how she could floor him for an absurd conclusion he had no right to have reached.

She could rise haughtily and stalk from the room. She could demand shrilly, How dared he? and What did he mean by——? But the nearby table, listening, was already too interested. Or she could—she caught her breath at the notion—she could encourage him to his jumped-at ideas about her, for the sheer enjoyment of his discomfiture when he learned the truth.

And that was — *Evening Out* was a bureau inaugurated by an enterprising peeress to provide unimpeachable social contacts for young professionals or business men temporarily in London without girls of their own class to escort to dinner or a theatre for an evening. Tara, at twenty-four, with several secretaryships behind her, had been on her last day of a temporary one with the bureau when she had volunteered to stand in for the society girl who found she was unable to keep the date arranged for her with Charlot Leloupblanc, a wine salesman with his family firm, in London on a selling trip.

Tara's boss had been grateful for her offer, and on that first meeting she had kept the bureau's strict rule as to both meetings and partings being at a public place, not at the girl's place of residence. This preserved her privacy and made each date a one-off affair which she need not repeat if she wished otherwise.

But when Tara and Charlot had taken at once to each other, and she had no further commitments to *Evening Out* in any capacity, they had continued to see each other often until tonight. It had developed into as normal and enjoyable an affair as might have happened in any other way. It was Dracon Leloupblanc who had chosen to see the whole set-up as squalidly commercial, though how Charlot had allowed him to get that impression, Tara could not think.

Anyway, he deserved to eat his own error at whatever future time he had to ... The thought served to put her on level terms with him, making it easier to eat the food and drink the wine he was providing. The rapiers were out between them ...

He was asking, 'Tell me, does your—association?—guild?—trade union?—encourage its clients and the attractive items of its stock-in-trade to go off hand-in-hand into the sunset as you and Charlot seem to have done? I'd have thought it would have preferred to provide the client with as much change as possible? This desirable girl tonight; that voluptuous one tomorrow. But I am wrong? It's not so?'

Tara played along. 'If a man wishes to see us again, we are free to agree or not. There's no rule against it,' she said.

'I see. You can play it by ear, as the saying goes?'

Surprised that he knew the idiom, she agreed. 'And if we both care to, we can go on from there,' she added, tempted to mention that very morning's wedding at St Margaret's, Westminster, between a wealthy young German politician and a baronet's daughter, who had met through the bureau. But she refrained.

Dracon murmured, 'As you and Charlot "went on from there". And does the profession pay well?'

Tara thought of the salary an experienced secretary could command and said, 'Very well.'

His eyes studied the soft draping of her gown, lingered on the swell of her breasts which she knew it revealed. 'With dress and cosmetic allowance included or extra?' he suggested.

(Like luncheon vouchers? Less angered than she was, she might have laughed.) 'No, these we provide ourselves,' she told him gravely.

He nodded and changed the subject. 'I understand Charlot had invited you to meet his family at Isray? He will have described who and how we are there?

And you have accepted his invitation?'

'For a holiday, I had, yes. But——'

'You may take a holiday from your—work, as you wish?'

'I am at the end of one contract and I am free until I take another,' she said with truth.

'With an eye to bettering yourself next time, as in domestic service?' he insinuated.

He could imply insolence without uttering a single openly offensive word! Suddenly Tara had had enough of the cross-talk she had invited. She shook her head as the desserts trolley was brought. He dismissed it. 'You will take a liqueur with your coffee?'

'No, thank you. And no coffee. I was going to say just now that though I had told your cousin I would go to Isray for a short holiday, naturally I shan't be going now——'

'No? Why not?'

Tara ignored that. She picked up her bag from the table. 'I must go.'

He lingered to pay the bill and caught up with her as she was collecting her wrap from the cloakroom. At the entrance he told the doorman, 'My car, please,' and Tara added to the man, 'And a taxi for me.'

Her companion promptly countermanded the order. 'I am using a hired car. I shall see you home,' he said.

'Oh no, that's not necessary at all.'

He merely confirmed to the man, 'No taxi for Madame,' and, short of brawling with him, there was nothing she could do but stand beside him in silence until his car was brought up.

He put her into it, tipped the doorman and took the wheel. 'What address?' he asked.

'Hampstead.' She gave him the road and her number. 'It's the N.W. district.'

'Thanks, but I am often enough in London on business to know my way about. Your address is a house? An apartment?'

'A flat in a modern block on the edge of the Heath.'

'The rent coming on your expenses account, no doubt?'

'No. The tenancy is mine.'

His head turned briefly towards her. 'You surprise me. Shouldn't accommodation be an understood perquisite of the job, along with transport and drinks too perhaps?'

She had a mental image of an office chief's reaction to being presented with an expenses sheet for such things. 'It's not very usual practice,' she said, which he accepted with a 'Not so? Too bad.'

Next he was asking, 'I am wondering why, after dinner, you were proposing to scuttle home alone in a taxi? Surely——?'

'And *I* am wondering, *monsieur*, why you should have expected me to do otherwise?' she cut in. 'You thrust your company on me for dinner, but I can't see that my allowing that entitled you to escort me home. I'd also be interested to know why, after ensuring that your cousin shouldn't be seeing me again, you troubled to meet me yourself?' she challenged.

A pause, then Dracon answered obliquely, 'Charlot

came to London to do business. A firm's time otherwise occupied is money wasted. Which is why I chose
to see for myself in whose tempting company it was
being wasted—if it was. Hence my keeping tonight's
rendezvous with you in Charlot's place. You see?'

'With his consent that you should?'

'I didn't consult him.'

'Knowing he wouldn't agree to such interference in
his affairs?'

'Knowing that, as he is my salaried employee, his
agreement was neither here nor there. My decision to
come to meet you myself was my own, in the interests
of the very justifiable curiosity I've mentioned. That
was why I came.'

'Overriding Charlot, giving him orders——'

'As I thought, he has already persuaded you of my
tyranny!'

'Despatching him, like a disobedient puppy to his
kennel. He is twenty-three, an adult! But you assume
the right to check up on him and see with your own
eyes the kind of harpy you think has ensnared him,
don't you? Well, I hope your inspection of me is
satisfied!' Tara raged.

On a short mirthless laugh Dracon said, 'The chink
in my armour—admitting to curiosity about you! But
yes, I certainly endorse Charlot's enthusiasm as to your
chic, your poise, your enviable vital statistics——'

'Thank you.' She hoped her deliberate drawl of the
words might imply an unspoken 'for nothing', and that
he would read the sarcasm behind it. But he merely
went on, 'Though in the circumstances you can hardly

expect me to appreciate all the other qualities he attributes to you; all those unmatched excellencies which he sees *couleur de rose*, without a flaw, and which has led him, he tells me, to ask you to marry him. For this, I think you may agree, *madame*, is a state of affairs which we cannot have?' he concluded on a low, insinuating note, assuming he had her agreement to a decision *he* had made, a decision about something which was entirely fresh and startling news to her.

Charlot hadn't proposed to her! It must be another wrong impression Dracon had gained. But seeing the advantage to her befooling of him of letting him believe it, she asked, 'You are saying that, considering the way Charlot and I met, *you* couldn't have it?'

He nodded. 'You take my point exactly.'

'With a full right to veto it, I suppose?'

'With enough authority to ensure that Charlot does not marry without my consent, yes. Which of course he knows.'

'I see. And I'm to understand that your authority extends also to forbidding me to accept Charlot's invitation to his home?'

Tara had assumed she need hardly ask the question, and was taken aback when he replied blandly, 'No, I see no reason why that should not go through. Charlot may be hoping of it more than he should, but as a holiday for you, I shouldn't care to deny it to you. You will go to Isray as you planned?'

Though Tara told herself that nothing in the world would drag her to France with his patronising consent, by the rules of the game she was playing, she decided to leave him guessing.

'Perhaps,' she told him distantly.

'You have already told Charlot that you would,' he reminded her.

'That was before I knew I was to be vetted and rejected by the head of his family. Since then I'm having second thoughts.'

'Though I doubt if you will listen to them. My bizarre intervention in your affair with Charlot; his dramatised version of my despotism; your spirited need to defend him from it—all these will have whetted your curiosity and your appetite for a social environment that is somewhat beyond your ken, and yes, I think you will decide to come to Isray, *madame*,' he asserted.

To which Tara longed to retort that if he was a Leloupblanc, *she* was a Dryden, related through her dead father to the ancient kings of Ireland, and that she had no need to peer from her gutter to see how the other half lived. But instead she allowed her silence to tell him neither yes nor no.

She had to direct him for the last part of the drive to her apartment. He went into the entrance hall with her and saw her to her door on the ground floor. She used her key and turned to face him, deciding that a curt goodnight should dismiss him. But he lingered.

'Am I to believe this is as far as you allowed Charlot to go?' he asked.

'After our first meeting he used to see me home.'

'I see. And naturally would be invited in—for coffee?' As Tara saw Dracon's hand go to an inner pocket of his jacket and draw out his wallet, she realised too late where her duping of him had led her —to the ultimate humiliation which she guessed he had in mind as he fingered some banknotes.

'Would Charlot have settled with you in cash, or through an account with your—er—sponsors?' he asked. And when, watching his flicking fingers in horror, she made no reply, he added impatiently, 'Oh, really! Please don't pretend we can be delicate about this. I have monopolised an evening which you might have occupied much more profitably. And so——?'

Tara had only herself to blame for encouraging him in his judgment of her as a tramp, but she could not take this final blatant insult. Her hand shot the wallet from his grasp and his sardonic face was the target of her ready open palm.

It made no contact. His lightning snatch at her wrist twisted it painfully as he stooped to retrieve his wallet, and when he straightened there was a dark threat in his eyes. By means of the wrist he still held he thrust that arm behind her back and drew her so close that her stiff resistant body was aligned to his.

'I'd have thought your professional experience would have taught you that fisticuffs of that sort tend only to inflame a man. Be careful, or you could find me claiming full value for my money!' he warned her.

'You wouldn't dare, and I wouldn't touch your money if—if——' she panted.

'And I wouldn't spend it to sample your secondhand favours. So don't worry—you aren't going to suffer my brutish embrace in lieu of Charlot's lovemaking tonight,' he retorted. 'But I've occupied time which might have meant cash to you, and so, however crude you seem to find the question—how much?'

For answer she struggled and bent in an effort to free herself from his hold. But she did not succeed, and had to await his contemptuous release of her. Then, through gritted teeth, 'Please leave!' she ordered him, and waited.

He did not hurry. He put away his wallet, flicked an imaginary speck from his sleeve and offered her his hand.

She ignored it and put meaning emphasis into her repeated, 'Good*night, monsieur*.' He replied with as casual an '*Au revoir*' as if they would be meeting again. Then he turned and left her.

The doors to the outer hall swung to behind him and she heard the engine of his car start up before she went into the apartment.

She should have been heady with the success of her deception of him. But the raw crudity of those last few minutes with him had drained her of all triumph. *He* had won, she had not; his threat something to be feared, but his scornful rejection of her 'secondhand favours' the ultimate affront he could offer her. The shame of the memory was going to rankle for ever.

The routine of her everyday had to assert itself. At the

moment she had no other post in view and she was going to miss the times she had enjoyed with Charlot before he had proved such a craven. But as she would not now be going to France, she began to debate the kind of job she would look for next. Temporary secretaries were in demand and with the French and German she had acquired in a year of *au pair* situations after leaving school she could take correspondence in both languages. Her last post before the one at *Evening Out* had been with an export firm, and she would be welcome there again, she knew.

But her letter approaching the managing director was not to be written. She was putting away her purchases after a morning's shopping when her doorbell rang and she opened to Dracon Leloupblanc.

He bowed. 'May I come in?'

Her frown covered her dismay at sight of him. 'Must you?' she asked coldly. 'What do you want?'

'A word with you. A suggestion. Please——?'

Reluctantly she stood aside for him and followed him into her living-room, where she did not invite him to sit. He turned to her. 'You are still between contracts?' he asked. 'Or are you engaged in a new one?'

'Not yet, but——'

'Ah, then you are free to come to Isray on the invitation my cousin made you,' he cut in.

'You can't be serious!' Her stare was incredulous. 'I haven't given another thought to it. And anyway, you forbade it.'

'I haven't forbidden the visit—only the outcome

Charlot would have been hoping for when he asked you to marry him and to meet his family. And as long as *you* understand there's no question of its leading to marriage, there seems no reason why you shouldn't accept.'

'After the judgment you'd made of me even before you'd met me? You're wasting your time, *monsieur*, suggesting I would accept Isray's hospitality on condition that I kept your cousin at arm's length while I was there. And as if, after the way you interfered between us, *he* could still hope there could be any future for our affair!' Tara scoffed.

She watched Dracon's cynical mouth curve upward in a half-smile. 'You conclude then that, because I can order his movements, I can also control the caprice of his heart? I am not God, *madame*, after all!' he countered drily, adding, 'And please spare me the retort of "You surprise me," for I can read the thought in your face!'

Tara ignored the gibe. 'You're saying that though Charlot had to obey when you sent him back home, he's still of the same mind about me?' she asked slowly, giving herself time to catch and hold on to an idea which had flicked across her mind.

'Fantasy-ridden to the point of idolatry, I'm afraid! A state of affairs which, if only for the sake of his use as an employee, I can tolerate for only just so long,' Dracon said.

'And yet you're suggesting that we should meet

each other again? What could that do to cure him of being in love with me?'

'It could well succeed where I shall continue to fail while he still has hopes of you,' Dracon admitted. 'In his present infatuation he is not going to take your No through anyone's proxy, least of all mine. He is not going to take your refusal of him except from you, face to face.' Dracon's hands spread expressively. 'That, *madame*, is my case.'

As he spoke Tara sensed a moment of power over him. For the first and only time he was asking, not ordering, and the thread of her idea which had rounded into a resolve, was going to respond. *But not as he expected. Not as he wanted!* She said slowly, as if she had to work it out, 'You think Charlot will only take it from me in person that the whole thing is over between us?' And then, forestalling Dracon's reply, 'But aren't you assuming rather too readily that it's quite as simple as that; that *my* feelings for *him* are of no account?'

Dracon's flecked eyes, insolent as ever, met hers in a basilisk stare. 'Need we consider your emotions for a moment?' he drawled. 'My cousin Charlot was only your client for an idle evening or two, was he not?'

That clinched it. The details of her plan had yet to be knitted into a pattern, but when they were, there were going to be no loose ends.

'Very well, I'll go to Isray,' she said.

CHAPTER TWO

BEFORE she could change her mind Tara had booked a flight to Bordeaux, had shopped for clothes and selected and packed the more attractive ones she had.

On that morning of her decision Dracon had advised against her telling Charlot she was going, and sure as she was that Dracon had no inkling as to her own plan, she did not argue. Let him think he was masterminding the whole thing! It wasn't going to be her fault if he didn't soon learn how wrong he was.

He believed she had fallen in with his suggestion, whereas, for the period of her visit to Isray, she was going to encourage Charlot with all the charm she could muster. It was possible that as soon as Dracon realised she was defying him he might create an ugly scene and ask her to leave. But meanwhile she would have given him some bad moments. And though she was going to feel guilty at using Charlot as a pawn in her game against Dracon, it was also possible that she might find she was not acting a part. Now she was despising Charlot for his weak subservience to Dracon, and she was not in love with him, but his eager pleasure in her company had had an infectious appeal which she had not tried to resist. Brief as their affair had been, it had had the makings of love in it, and

perhaps she hadn't the right to judge Charlot's reaction to Dracon's dominant authority. For within
minutes of meeting him and against her will, hadn't
she bent to it herself?

She flew to Bordeaux on a golden May afternoon.
Dracon was waiting for her with a porter when she had
collected her luggage from the carousel and they followed the man to his parked car.

He was wearing a dark blue open-necked shirt with
light grey trousers of raw silk, the informality of both
a complete contrast to the correct London clothes in
which she had previously seen him. Sleeves rolled high
above his elbows revealed sinewed arms deeply tanned,
and his hands upon the steering wheel brought a
memory of the strength with which one of them had
pinioned and held her helpless until he had chosen to
let her go. This was the same assured man of that
evening, but somehow less urbane, more virile, more
... animal, the despoiling wolf of his name, but a black
wolf, not a white. Walking beside him and seated with
him in the car, Tara had an odd feeling of being as
acutely aware of him as she was of herself. And there
was something almost frightening about that.

He drove south-east into country which Charlot
had described to her, a region of neat vineyards and
small hamlets, with the blue water of the Garonne to
be glimpsed in the distance. The Château d'Isray,
though nearly an hour's drive from the airport, was no
more than twelve kilometres from the southern border
of the city and had now no working vineyards attached

to it. As Dracon drove out to it he explained why to
Tara, who welcomed the impersonal subject as a fillgap
of time alone with him of which she had been nervous.

'The land is there,' he said, 'fifty potentially pro-
ductive hectares of it, but the owners went bankrupt
some years back, and the estate and the château went
to the principal creditor. We Leloupblancs have always
been shippers only, but my father bought the house
from this man, and would have made a deal for the
land too if he hadn't died suddenly, and his daughter,
Ninon Chauvet, has consistently refused either to sell
it or develop it. When her father sold us the château
he kept the dower house on the estate, and Ninon lives
in it, our nearest neighbour. You will meet her.'

Making conversation, Tara asked, 'Would you still
buy if she would sell?'

Dracon nodded. 'Willingly. There is no reason why
there shouldn't be a Château d'Isray Graves of the
premier class, but while Ninon won't name a price for
the estate, that must remain something for the future.'

So there was someone at least who could defy his
will, thought Tara, feeling admiration for the unknown woman who had done it. Aloud she said mischievously, 'And so far you have found no way of
forcing her hand? You surprise me, Monsieur Leloupblanc, you really do!'

He ignored the mockery in her tone. 'Dracon, please,
within the family,' he corrected, adding, 'But yes,
sometimes I surprise myself that I haven't tried harder
with Ninon until now.'

'Confident, I suppose, that if you had tried harder, you could get your way?' she prompted tartly.

He shot her a quick glance. 'As I guessed, Charlot has schooled you well as to my character! And so, yes again. For there are always means of persuading a woman into the way one wants her to go. One need only find the particular spur to which she will respond, and, as with a mare, she is one's own from then on.'

'But you haven't yet found the right spur for Mademoiselle?—Madame?—Chauvet?'

'For Ninon, for want of trying, not yet. But I am biding my time,' he said.

He slowed the car for the entrance to a drive leading to a house of many deep windows, each flanked by green shutters against white stone walls, dappled in the early evening sunlight by the shadows of the branches of the trees bordering an opposite lawn. There was a porticoed entrance door reached by broad steps; inside, where Dracon led the way, a cool, dark hall and a graceful wide staircase, and beyond, open french doors leading to the contrasting lightness of a square, paved court, its centrepiece a playing fountain, with raised flowerbeds, massed with colour, radiating from it. There were more flowers and shrubs in beds bordering the wings of the house which enclosed the courtyard on all four sides. There were seats there and a couple of sun umbrellas shading tables on which there were bottles and glasses, and people, and talk which suddenly stilled as Dracon showed Tara out from the house.

As her eyes adjusted to the brightness after the dark of the hall, Tara saw that the people were a middle-aged woman with a doll-like pink and white complexion and slightly greying hair, a suntanned fair girl, stretched on a garden lounger, the fingers of one drooping hand idly trailing the stone coping of the fountain, a third woman, thin-faced, with a swathe of brown hair twisted into a ballet knot, wearing an emerald green shirt and Bermuda shorts rolled up to reveal slim legs and ankles crossed on the rungs of a nearby chair—and Charlot, lithe and easy-limbed, using the edge of a table for a seat.

While he and Tara were still in the shadow of the house, Dracon murmured, 'My aunt Mathilde, Elaine Dorsay, Ninon Chauvet,' by way of introduction of the women, before his aunt, rising, exclaimed in French, 'Dracon! We were not expecting you——!' and Charlot, straightening and staring, loped forward, hands outstretched.

'Tara! How——?' But his question dropped away and he halted as if stricken to stone as Dracon came forward into the sunlight, drawing Tara beside him, his forearm closely aligned to hers and her hand in a vice-like grip from which she could not wrench free.

Holding me as intimately as if he owned me, or were laying claim to me! was her instant, resentful thought, as the smile she had had ready for Charlot in defiance of him froze on her lips when she heard him inviting the others, 'Tante Mathilde, Ninon, Elaine— meet Mademoiselle Tara Dryden, my English fiancée of a very few days!'—an announcement which could not have stunned even Charlot more than it had appalled her.

She pulled far enough away from Dracon's side to turn to look at him, horrified denial ready on her tongue. But the deep thrust of his nails into the soft flesh of her palm was enough of agony to keep her silent, even without his muttered 'Tais-toi!'—a warning to be quiet with which he might have threatened a child.

Like a film in slow motion his news took effect upon his hearers. His aunt, twittering surprise and congratulations to him, ran to embrace Tara on both cheeks. Elaine Dorsay smiled—she had a sweet, open smile—and beckoned to him. Ninon Chauvet's expression was unreadable by Tara. A spot of hectic colour appeared on each high cheekbone of her thin face and she allowed herself an enigmatic Mona Lisa smile, without showing or voicing surprise or the curiosity with which the older woman was bubbling over. As for Charlot—after one long aghast stare at Tara, he muttered some oaths under his breath, then strode past her and Dracon into the house and away.

Ninon Chauvet commented drily, 'He does not like your choice of wife, my friend. Or he is jealous of you —who knows?' To which Dracon replied, 'He is a young boor without manners,'—a cruelty for which Tara longed to strike him.

He went to Elaine and sat on the end of her sun lounger. 'You are happy for us?' he asked.

'Very happy.' She put out a hand to Tara, and not knowing that Tara had understood the French being spoken, managed in careful English, 'I am glad that you are to be one of us, *mademoiselle*. Welcome to Isray!'

'Spoken like the best phrase-book!' Dracon praised her, then asked, 'Have you been into the pool today?'

Elaine shook her head. 'No, the water was too cold.'

'Riding, then?'

'Charlot would not come with me. Besides, I was tired.'

Dracon frowned and stood up. 'You know she is supposed to do both every day. Why didn't you order Charlot to go riding with her?' he asked his aunt, standing by with Tara.

Mathilde's face crumpled. 'I could not command him,' she said timidly. 'Since you sent him back from England he is in a mood. He sulks and broods. You saw for yourself just now—he hadn't a word of congratulation for you, and Mademoiselle Dryden might have been invisible to him!'

'Or too attractively visible, perhaps?' The murmur came from Ninon Chauvet as she rose and stretched as gracefully as a cat. 'I must go,' she said, and approaching Dracon, tapped him intimately upon his chest. 'You must bring your surprise packet to the Dower House to see me very soon,' she told him, and then with a thin smile added to Tara in English, 'And you, *mademoiselle*, must tell how you managed to capture

him, when the whole of our sex in the region has failed
—so far!'

When she had gone, after waving airily to Mathilde
and Elaine, Tara realised that since Dracon had made
his outrageous, lying announcement, she herself had
not spoken a word. But what could she say to these
people who believed him? And what now was she
going to say to Charlot when they met? *He* couldn't
believe—could he?—that she had fallen to what must
have been a lightning courtship by Dracon, if it had
happened? And why, *why* had Dracon claimed it?
She couldn't wait to know.

She saw now that Elaine had risen from the sun
lounger and was standing. But not naturally, not fully
upright. She was bent sideways from the right hip,
and when she began to walk towards the house it was
with the aid of a stick. She was, even if only temporarily, a partial cripple. Yet neither Charlot nor
Dracon, thought Tara compassionately, had described
her so. The omission seemed odd, and again Tara
wondered why.

An hour later she had been assigned a pleasant ground-
floor room looking on to the lawns and flowers of a
side garden, and she had established with Mathilde
that she spoke and understood enough French as to
surprise and please that lady.

'Dracon and Charlot need the English for their business, you understand,' she said. 'Elaine and I have
only *un petit peu*—a very little. Myself, I do not travel

far, and she cannot, *la pauvre*.'

Tara had asked then about Elaine, and had heard that in her earlier teens she had had polio, and now, under physiotherapy care, it was hoped she might achieve a measure of recovery in time.

'But she must exercise; she must walk, she must ride, she must swim. Dracon has added a quiet mare to his stable for her, and she should use the swimming-pool every day,' Mathilde explained. 'And when she does not, he is angry, as you saw,' she concluded with a sigh.

The family dined at eight, ('very simply, unless Dracon is entertaining business guests', according to Mathilde) and as Tara changed for it she was re-hearsing the showdown she planned to stage with Dracon before it. Alone with him for a few minutes when they had left the courtyard for the house, she had meant to demand it, but he had forestalled her. 'On the terrace outside your room,' he had told her curtly. 'At seven. I shall be there.'

She changed into a blouson dress of white crêpe with batwing sleeves clasped into a cuff above the elbow. It was one of her new purchases bought with Charlot in mind, but it was of Dracon that she was thinking—of how he had tricked her into coming to Isray for the purpose of turning Charlot down, when he had been plotting this extraordinary claim to her himself. True, in her turn she had meant to trick him, but could he have guessed, when she had fallen in with his suggestion, that she had hatched some counterplot? Was she then so transparent? Or he so uncannily perceptive as to have foreseen how her mind had been working against him?

It seemed that he had. When she drew back the curtains of her window and stepped on to the twilit terrace outside, he was there and said immediately to her questioning look, 'You are asking yourself a big Why, I can see. And so—you didn't suppose I was going to allow you to come here, only to bewitch Charlot all over again? For that was your idea, was it not?'

She wouldn't give him the satisfaction of hearing he was right. She evaded his question. 'It was you who suggested my coming, and persuaded me that I should,' she accused him.

He smiled faintly. 'Ah, but not for the reason I gave you. I'm not so naïve as to expect you to have accepted that at its face value. Which is why, when you appeared to agree, I knew you must have some other plan in mind.'

Stung, she retorted, 'If you're as certain as that, there's no use in my supposing you would believe me if I denied it——'

'No use at all,' he agreed, looking her over with lazy insolence. 'You are dressing too desirably to be able to deny it is for some man's attention, and if not for Charlot's, then for whose?'

She ignored the barb in the pseudo-compliment. 'I dress to please myself,' she snapped.

'The veil of half-truth behind which all women hide! Or am I perhaps taking too narrow a view, and your exquisite grooming is a tool of your professional experience, designed for the attraction of any man in sight, anyone at all? Even—incredibly enough—for mine?' he insinuated.

She flared at that. 'You're despicable as well as a cheat,' she declared. 'You brought me here to break with Charlot face to face, when I could have done it by letter just as well——'

'I couldn't trust either you to do it by letter, or him to accept it.'

'Then why should he accept it by word of mouth from me?'

Feigning patience with obtuseness, Dracon said, 'I've told you already that the reason I gave you wasn't my real one.'

'Exactly! Cheating me into coming, as I've said!'

'You came for your own reasons, not mine, my dear. You show a pretty turn of cheating yourself,' he retorted.

That it was true—she *had* tried to cheat him— did nothing to soothe her sense of outrage against him. 'You! You! *You* had your reasons; *you* didn't trust me; *you* couldn't leave Charlot to know his own mind!' she raged. 'So who *are* you, Dracon Leloupblanc, that you think you can arrange and manage and puppet-string everyone you know? Just who *are* you? Tell me that!'

With infuriating calm, 'I am Dracon Leloupblanc,' he said.

'And——?'

'And so, as with your Celtic clans the head of the family is "The" McAirdrie, "The" Macdonagh, I am "Leloupblanc", the head of mine.'

'Which entitles you to——?'

'To direct it in the way I want it to go. My family, I'd remind you, derives from the time when wolves, black, white, brown or brindle, did roam France, giving point to the saying "Where the he-wolf leads, the pack will follow"——our family's motto, by the way. You understand who I am now, *madame*? And that I can usually find methods of getting my way?'

Tara nodded tautly. 'As you've done with me——telling me one thing, meaning another. Though I'd like to remind you, *I'm* not a member of your pack!'

'You chose to involve with it when you encouraged Charlot and planned to beguile him again. You can't avoid the consequences of that.'

'In other words, *you* mean to see that I don't!' she sneered. 'So what was your reason which you kept back from me?'

He looked away across the garden and his answer, when it came, seemed entirely out of context. 'You have seen Elaine Dorsay—how she is?' he asked.

Puzzled, 'Yes, that she's lame,' Tara said. 'Madame Leloupblanc told me——'

'But Charlot didn't tell you that he and Elaine are as good as engaged; that their betrothal has been an understood thing between them since their childhood?' Dracon, watching Tara closely now, must have been gratified by her long-drawn breath of dismay.

'No. *No!*' she denied. 'Of course he told me of her,

as he did of you and his mother. But no details about her. Not that she was crippled. Nor—nor this.'

'Which is as one expected. Courting you, he would hardly confess to being committed in honour to her, would he?' Dracon queried. 'But you understand now why I really brought you over? In order that you might see for yourself the havoc you have wreaked in her life and in his. Or to put it another way, to shame you into breaking with him, which I didn't believe you ever intended to do—a Leloupblanc of the Château d'Isray being too good a catch for a woman of your background, I argued. Also to shame him into enough compassion for Elaine to let you go; even to send you away.'

'That won't be necessary. I'm leaving now, as soon as I can.'

He shook his head slowly. 'If it were only as simple as that!'

'It is as simple at that,' Tara insisted. 'I have only to pack and go. I'd never forgive myself if I came between Charlot and Elaine in the circumstances. And in going, I shall be leaving you to deal with the havoc *you've* created by claiming to your family that we're engaged!' she added spitefully.

'As you say, you would be leaving me to it *if* you were going at once—which you are not. I'm afraid you underrate me sadly if you think Leloupblanc is to be put in the position of claiming a woman in betrothal, only for her to reject him publicly one, two or three days later——'

'Very well,' she cut in. 'I'll make it four days ahead,

if that will do anything for the Leloupblanc pride. That is, I'll break it off after I've gone. But I am going—tonight if that's possible. At latest, tomorrow, and you can think of some reason for my having been "unexpectedly called away".'

'No!' He barked the forbidding word at her. 'No, if and when the rejection is made, you can't count on my chivalry to allow you to make it; it will have to be by our common consent. Meanwhile, the engagement stays and you stay with it.'

'You can't expect me to go along with that lie!' she protested. 'For one thing, from the little time you were in London after you sent Charlot home, your people must know we can hardly even have met.'

Dracon shrugged. 'No problem. Mutual attraction can happen overnight, as Charlot's infatuation for you seems to have done. And as he won't have confessed to Elaine the reason for his abrupt return, they can believe he introduced us to each other before he left.'

'Then how does he explain his behaviour when you told them? His shock at seeing me and his—his hurt? You saw him and heard him,' Tara accused.

'If he is concerned to keep the truth from Elaine, he will have to explain it. For instance, he could heartily dislike you and disapprove of you for me. That should serve. And yes, I do expect your co-operation, if only to prove you are not lying when you claim that for your life's sake you wouldn't come between those two, knowing what you do about Elaine.'

'Nor would I, though I only know that you've told

me they're promised to each other. No more than that,' Tara pointed out.

Dracon said emphatically, 'Then you can take it from me that before you happened to Charlot the "promising" was mutual and that Elaine has loved him ever since she learned what the word means. Also you must take it that, since she must have no chance to suspect anything between you and Charlot, our pre-occupation with each other must appear complete. And also again——' in the pause which he allowed to stretch out, Tara sensed a dynamism, an intensity of will which frightened her—'*also*,' he repeated, 'if I am to trust your sincerity in making amends, *you* are going to convince Charlot of the reality of our engagement to the point where he will lose all hope of you or come to despise you. Either or both will serve my purpose. You understand?'

Dared she defy him? She wished she believed she could. 'You plotted all this before you brought me here?' she asked.

'Say, rather, that I added it as a strength to my original plan to show you how things were with Elaine, and to hope you would feel for her.'

Bitterly, 'You couldn't trust me so far without forc-ing my hand?'

'I couldn't then. Can I now? You will stay and go along with me in it? On my conditions, not your own this time?'

She looked away. 'I—suppose so.'

'Good. Though if I may take that half-hearted admission as consent, perhaps we had better discuss practicalities. Can you afford to stay?'

'Afford to?' she echoed, puzzled.

'Well, can you? I don't forget that in your line of work, your time means money. So if your co-operation is going to embarrass you financially, you have only to name your price.'

Though she should be used to his gratuitous insults by now, Tara gasped. 'You're trying to bribe me?' she demanded.

'Bribe? No. You have already agreed to stay. I was merely offering to buy your services at the current market price,' he corrected.

'Which you've already done once before, if you remember?'

He nodded. 'I remember, and that your answer was an outraged and virtuous No.'

'Good. For it's the same now—*No!*'

'As you please, though I reserve the right to look at the possibilities of an expenses account,' he murmured, then looked at his watch. 'It's time we were joining the others for dinner.' He offered her his hand.

Nothing would induce her to take it. 'I'm not quite ready. Please go without me,' she said.

'Very well.' But on the point of stepping back into the garden, he turned. 'Tante Mathilde tells me something I hadn't learned about you—that you understand and speak French fluently. Do you?' he asked.

'Reasonably well, I think,' she told him, her tone aloof.

WHERE THE WOLF LEADS

'As of course I might have guessed for myself,' he agreed. 'After all, at your level of operation, you must frequently entertain quite a cosmopolitan clientele—the cream of executive Paris, Berlin, Rome and even further afield. Isn't it so?'

And this was the man she had agreed to abet in acting a lie for the furthering of his own ends! Tara raged inwardly when he had left her. What had happened to her? To her will, to her pride, her self-respect? He boasted of leading, but he didn't lead—he bulldozed his way. Or no, that wasn't so either. He had neither led nor bulldozed, but manipulated rather —which was infinitely more subtle, more deadly.

She had fought him with words, but always in the end had yielded to the imposition of *his* will, even while deluding herself that her decisions were her own. He knew to a hair's breadth the value of the hinted threat, the smoothly turned insult, the equally silken false flattery. Without knowing her at all, he *knew* her, she felt, in every way which he could turn to his purpose, whereas she, as she had sensed earlier in the car, was equally aware of and alert to him, to his power with her, to a magnetic pull as ruthless and inevitable as that of the moon upon the tides.

The thought that he would expect to touch her or kiss her in front of other people in order to prove their supposed intimacy, sent a shiver of apprehensive excitement down her spine. If he did, could she bear it, or pretend to respond? Something of that inner awareness of him warned her that he would not stand for

pretence. But that she could ever feel or show passion
for Dracon Leloupblanc was a possibility that was out
of this world …

Charlot did not appear at dinner, for which Tara was
thankful. She would have to see him some time, she
knew, but if he did not contrive a meeting alone with
him, she must. She could not sit across a dinner-table
from him and behave as if she hardly knew him. Nor,
she suspected, would he do the same.

The talk, over a light meal of an iced soup, fish
salad and fresh fruit, was in French, most of which
she understood and was able to join in. Mathilde
Leloupblanc wanted news of London which she knew
slightly. She also questioned Tara as to her background
and her family, to hear that her father, a widower and
an Army officer, had gone back to his native Ireland
to spend his retirement, but had recently died. She had
no other close relatives.

'Then perhaps, if you have no one very close to you,
you will be happy to be married to Dracon from here,'
Mathilde hoped aloud, though needing to glance at
Dracon for his agreement to the idea, Tara noticed.

'And you were working in London when you met
Dracon?' Mathilde asked next. 'You have connections
or friends in the English wine industry?'

'No.' Tara looked straight at Dracon as she added
carefully, 'Lately I have been working as a temporary
secretary to different firms, and Dracon and I happened to meet at dinner one night.'

'Since when she has found me under her feet at both inconvenient as well as convenient moments,' he told Mathilde drily, appearing to accept Tara's flat statement as to her work as if she had said nothing to surprise him.

Mathilde uttered a small sound which might have been a sigh. 'Ah, whirlwind and domineering as ever, you,' she accused him, then added more brightly, 'However, that you did not allow Tara to escape you is a good thing. We are going to be glad about that, are we not, Elaine *chérie*?' she appealed, drawing the girl into the conversation for almost the first time.

Elaine said, 'Yes.' And then abruptly, to Tara, 'Charlot was in London before Dracon went over this time. Did you know Charlot too?'

With no clue as to how to answer this, Tara hesitated and Dracon spoke for her. 'Yes, they had met once or twice. In fact, though he was prevented from making it, he was to have been one of the restaurant party where Tara and I met.'

Elaine addressed Tara again. 'But if he knew you, why did he behave so rudely when Dracon introduced you to us?'

'I—don't—know.'

'Though it is easy to guess,' Dracon interposed again. 'At some point or other she must have snubbed him for the young boor he can be. She doesn't know how, but if he is not man enough to forgive and forget, he is going to have to answer to me, be very sure.'

Elaine's face clouded. 'He is *not* a boor,' she muttered under her breath.

'Not in your eyes, perhaps.'

She looked up, her mouth working. 'Except when you make him one! As you also make him out to be an idler and a sponger, which he is *not*,' she defended Charlot.

'Only because I keep him up to the mark in his work and his duty to you. For example, why didn't he take you riding today?'

'You know that Filoselle is sick.'

Dracon's brows lifted. 'Still?'

'Yes. Jacques says she is getting better, but Charlot is still worried and he goes to see her in her box every night and morning—before he goes to bed and as soon as he is up.'

'Nevertheless, there are the other mares he could ride. If you go on Dansette, he could take Chasseuse d'Or. So I shall expect to hear tomorrow that you have been out together as usual. You understand?'

Elaine compressed her lips and made no reply. Tara, glancing at Mathilde, saw her look of distress for the girl, as if she knew from experience that any such clash of wills always ended in the crumbling of Elaine's defiance. Fortunately, this time, she could rise from the table, which she did, and they went to the salon for coffee.

Dracon drank one demi-tasse, then excused himself. When he had gone Mathilde sighed, 'I should have thought he would want to spend your first evening with you, my dear. But this is his way—to work in his study after dinner——' She paused. 'Would you like me, perhaps, to remind him presently that he is neglecting you?'

From the relief on her face when Tara refused the offer, saying she was rather tired and would go to bed very soon, it was plain that Mathilde hadn't relished the prospect of bearding Dracon, and when, later, she wondered aloud where Charlot could be, saying she must question his churlishness before he had to face Dracon, Tara judged it time to make her escape to her room. The very last thing she wanted was to be present at an inquest on behaviour of which she knew the cause only too well.

How *did* Dracon hope to maintain the charade of their engagement in face of Charlot's almost certain rejection of its possibility? she wondered. Charlot wasn't going to believe she had switched loyalties so swiftly and easily, and yet her pledge to Dracon for Elaine's sake made it imperative she should try to convince him that she had—that Dracon was her chosen man, her destiny, only for the whole web of intrigue to be abandoned when Charlot conceded victory to Dracon and went back to Elaine. Poor Elaine! —no less a pawn than was Charlot to Dracon's manoeuvres on her behalf. No less a tool which he had chosen to use than was Tara herself. Had no one ever told that man that people weren't mere shapes to be pushed about on a board at the whim of a dictator like himself?

And yet—to do him the minimum of justice—had he acted merely on a whim of power? If she hadn't somehow convinced her of his deep concern for Elaine's happiness, would she ever have agreed to help him by acting her part? She hoped not, but how was she to know that in going along with him in this, she was not already falling into step with his 'pack', as subject to his will as they were? *Please* not, she begged her fate. Let me stay *myself*!

Mathilde had accompanied her to her room, had drawn curtains, checked that she had everything she needed, and had bidden her goodnight with a kiss on either cheek. But when she had gone and Tara had undressed, she drew back the curtains again and stood at the open french window, barefoot and in a pleated silk negligé over her filmy nightgown.

The night air was sweet with the scent of jasmine. Somewhere nearby there must be honeysuckle too. A light breeze stirred the leaves of a row of aspens across a lawn, and a crescent slip of moon stood out against the dark velvet of the sky. An enchanting night and an enchanting place for those who could be happy and carefree in it. But for the others——

What was that? Some large bird—a pigeon or a roosting pheasant—soared up from a tree with a clatter of foliage and a beat of wings which outdid the sound that had startled it. It settled noisily on another tree, leaving Tara unaware that the disturbance had been caused by someone's approach until Dracon stood beside her at the window.

'Oh——!' With a hand at her throat in shock, she stepped back into the room and he followed. No wonder she hadn't heard him coming, for his bare feet were in monks' sandals. For the rest, the wide sleeves of his knee-length robe fell back to reveal the sheen of dark hair on his arms, and the robe itself was open to its belted waist. He was even nearer to complete undress than she!

'You have no right——! What—what do you want?' she breathed.

Hands in the pockets of his robe, he rocked back on his heels. 'You should have waited to say goodnight,' he said.

'I didn't know when you would come back, or whether you would. Besides, Charlot might have come in, and I couldn't——'

'He has come back now.'

'You've seen him? Lied to him—about us?'

'No. He gave me no opportunity, and I didn't seek one. Having an idea, you see, that for him a practical demonstration could do more than even the most glib of lies.'

'A—demonstration?' she queried. 'What do you mean?'

Standing over her now, he was menace itself, and instinct had leaped to warn her even before he replied with a drawled, 'Something physical—like this,' and his arms, sheer muscular iron, went round her, pinning her so close that the little they both wore might have been nothing between her flesh and his. Dangerously aware of him, and fearing what he might attempt next, Tara tried scorn.

She strained back far enough to look into his face. 'Needing to practise? To rehearse? None too sure that when you tell your lies about our phoney lovemaking, Charlot is going to believe you?'

Dracon said, 'My dear, this is no trial run. It is opportunity being snatched—a live performance. Come——' One hand firm at her waist beneath the silk of her negligé, the other clasping her shoulder, he drew her to him again. His forward leg thrust between her knees and he bent her backwards, curving his body above her and looking down at her upturned face. The hand which had held her shoulder gathered the fall of the russet hair, using it as a rope to hold her fast until lingeringly, searchingly, his mouth found hers, making each deep pressure of his lips a seduction, a rape of all that her will should have withheld from him, even while a shaming, unbidden surge of her blood could not.

She sensed his triumph as she softened, yielded, though hating the power of his virility which was betraying her to him. He knew that the heat and demand of his kisses had put her senses in thrall to him, and his conceit might dare further—*was* daring further, until suddenly he lifted his head, signalling to her to listen.

Still imprisoned in his arms, she listened, and at the sound of the approaching footsteps to which he had alerted her, the panic of physical desire he had roused in her chilled and died.

'S-someone is coming! Don't——' she begged, struggling to free herself.

'Yes,' he said. 'Charlot. As in any well-planned coup, the timing is all——' and bending to her again, he took her lips with the same mastery as before.

Beyond the open window the footsteps had stopped, and for Tara understanding flashed. *Dracon had planned this. He had expected Charlot to come by!* His assault upon her had been 'a live performance' for Charlot's witnessing; the lighted room, seen from the darkness outside, had been the stage on which Charlot should see for himself the intimacy he had achieved with her. Could trickery go further?

The footsteps moved on, were running now. Dracon straightened and stood away from her. His cynical gesture as of dusting off his hands infuriated her, and she turned on him.

'You *meant* Charlot to see us, as if——'

'As if we were the lovers he will have concluded by now that we are. I in your room; you——' Dracon's glance raked her déshabille—'prepared for me. Yes— the unpalatable facts in full Technicolor being worth a whole bookful of words, you may agree?'

'Agree? Do you expect me to? And I suppose your plot began when you suggested Madame Leloupblanc should give me a ground-floor room? Did you?'

He shook his head. 'Not guilty there. We often find guests like a room within sight and reach of the garden in summer. No, but you'll have heard Elaine say that Charlot goes down to see his mare every night? Well, the way to the stables lies past your window, and so I decided to show him how far I have put you out of his reach. It should shorten our campaign considerably.'

'*Your* campaign!' Tara snapped. 'And in aid of it, you even found you could make yourself pretend to sample my secondhand favours?' she added nastily.

Dracon shrugged. 'One must suffer in a worthy cause——'

'Worthy! I should never have let you persuade me to stay!' she declared wildly.

'You stayed,' he said coldly. 'And if you are appealing for my pity, you are wasting your time. For the moment I have pity only for Elaine, and you and Charlot may have to learn the hard way just how far in aid of that I can go.'

She had turned her back on him. Over her shoulder she said, 'Please leave,' and then, 'I warn you, I'm going to see Charlot as soon as I——'

But she spoke to empty air. Dracon had gone.

CHAPTER THREE

AT the beginning of the night Tara had not been able to sleep, and towards morning she did not allow herself even to doze. For a long while after Dracon had left her she had listened in vain for Charlot's return from the stables. But in the end she had to conclude

that he must have got back into the house by some
other way, for he did not come near.

Elaine, however, had said he went down early in the
morning, so not long after first light Tara was dressed
and on watch at her french window. If she didn't come
past soon, she meant to find her way down to the
stables, hoping to meet him there.

By the cool light of day she could hardly believe in
the scene which Dracon had forced upon her. She
could almost better imagine Charlot's shock at seeing
them locked in embrace than she could credit the effect
it had had upon her own will and senses. The reined
passion which Dracon had pretended to feel for her
had come near to the approach she knew she would
have welcomed from a man who claimed to love her—
nothing tentative about it, expecting response and, to
her shame, getting it from the fire which it had fanned
in her veins.

Other men had courted her; very early in their affair
Charlot had kissed her and caressed her. But she had
never yet been physically moved as by the false ardour
of a man she had every reason to hate. When she did
love and was loved for herself, was she going to remember and compare those desires with the brief
ecstasy of body which she had known last night in her
enemy's arms? She prayed not.

When she heard and saw Charlot coming, she was
at a loss to know what to say to him. For Elaine's sake
she had to stand by her word to Dracon, yet must
assure Charlot that they were not already the lovers he

must think them after Dracon's planned display.

She stepped out into his path, halting him. 'Charlot! Last night——' she began.

His eyes' boyish sparkle which had first attracted her to him had died. 'What about last night?' he demanded stonily. 'You've engaged yourself to the man, haven't you? And who but a fool like me would expect you to have waited even so long to be prepared to jump into bed with him? Why, by now it's probably a habit!'

'Oh, Charlot, it's not like that! I don't—— We aren't——' She put two urgent hands upon his arm; he shook them off. 'Listen, we aren't lovers. I swear it!'

'Just good friends, hm?'

'Don't sneer!'

'And you didn't fall for him as soon as I was out of the way? And he didn't *get* me out of the way on purpose, so that he could take you from me—no?'

'That's absurd! Dracon had never seen me until after he'd sent you home and he came to the Hartford to tell me so.'

'And to make very sure I shouldn't get or keep the girl I wanted. How do they say it in American?— "pulling rank" on me—assuming, as always, that he can bring me to heel, and making doubly sure by stealing you himself. Not that he really wants you, don't think that—only to keep you away from me.'

This was where the lies had to begin. 'If I didn't

think he wanted me, I shouldn't have got engaged to him,' Tara said quietly.

'Huh! Believe that if you must,' Charlot scoffed. 'But you weren't there when he refused to believe me when I told him you weren't the *cocotte* he thought you. I told him you were a trained secretary with a couple of languages at the end of your tongue, and he only laughed nastily and said he admired you for the perfect cover-up—holding down one profession by day, while you moonlighted in a more rewarding one by night. He knew it was commonly done, he said, but he had never met one of your tribe to date.'

So that was why Dracon had shown no surprise when she had claimed the truth to Mathilde, thought Tara. He had heard Charlot's defence of her, but deliberately hadn't heeded it, and to judge by Charlot's sullen resentment of her, he didn't care now whether Dracon had been convinced or not. Well, neither did she, she resolved in a flash of defiance. She needn't care anything for his opinion of her; in fact, since he had guessed at and defeated her plan to encourage Charlot's infatuation, it might do a lot for her pride to know she had successfully deceived him over something else.

Charlot went on mercilessly, 'And even if he has changed his mind about you since, you needn't think you'll have an easy passage—Ninon Chauvet will see to that. She didn't show a gleam of shock at his news, but she'll bounce back like india-rubber once she's had time to map her plan of campaign.'

Tara remembered the sinuous, catlike grace and withdrawn smile of Ninon Chauvet. 'Why should she be interested?' she asked Charlot, though her feminine instinct told her.

'Because,' Charlot confirmed, 'she aspires to Dracon herself. She is older than he is by about seven years— she's forty-four, and though she has had to stand for his affairs with other women, this is the first time he's claimed to be engaged, and she's going to feel she can't waste any more time in finesse—she'll have to show her hand. Which will mean getting rid of you, and though I couldn't care less what you've invited from both of them, I'm warning you, you aren't going to like it.'

Tara said, 'You're very bitter. And I can't help thinking that if you really had begun to fall in love with me, you would care what happened to me.'

'Through your own doing, with your eyes open, after I had told you the kind of monster Dracon is? Why should I care?' he flung at her. 'Besides, even if you were only amusing yourself with me, you knew very well what I felt for you, for I told you often enough!'

'Though without any right to feel anything for me, had you?' Tara parried quietly.

He stared, his handsome face flushing darkly. 'No *right*? What do you mean?'

But she saw that he knew when she said, 'Elaine,' and nothing more.

'*Elaine!*' he echoed. 'Who told you, and what?' And then, 'As if I couldn't guess—Dracon, of course?'

Tara nodded. 'You had mentioned her as if she were just someone around your home, and I imagined you as brother and sister. But Dracon told me the truth——'

'About our "understanding"? But that's just a—a family idea. There's never been anything binding about it on either side.'

'Dracon told me that Elaine believes implicitly that there is, and that you're in love with her, as much as she is with you.'

'And so?' He looked away uncomfortably and then paused, frowning in thought. He turned back, his expression changed to scorn. 'And so, *and so*——' he repeated. 'Yes, it figures. You weren't in love with me, but you were willing to listen—to a Leloupblanc from a landed estate in the romantic Gironde—until a bigger fish, *the* Great White Wolf himself, came along with a tale about the first one being already bespoken to a lame girl at home. And you—well, weren't you lucky? *Two* of them in tow, and you now with a pious excuse for jilting the first and landing the other! Yes, you've played your catch very well, Tara Dryden, and I wish you joy of it.'

'Charlot, it doesn't have to make us enemies. You did deceive me about Elaine, but——'

'Deceive you! As if you ever let me get so far—a few kisses in taxis, a goodnight clinch, and then your door firmly closed on me. *I* was serious, you weren't, but I was a fool not to jump the gun and take you, as Dracon has been allowed to!'

Desperately, 'Charlot, he——'

But a pull on her wrist had jerked her towards him. She stumbled awkwardly; he braced her, but there was no way in which she could save herself from falling but by clinging to him, and before she could straighten he had pushed her chin upward and was kissing her with cold, compressed lips—a boy's angry protest, impotent to stir any blood.

That was how Dracon, strolling from under the sun-dappled shadow of the trees, came upon them. How could Tara have known he was an early morning walker? How could she have guessed her ambush of Charlot would end like this? Horrified by a guilt of which she was innocent, she wrenched free of Charlot, ran back into her room, slammed and locked the french window, drew its curtains and ran to lock her room door.

Panting, she sank upon her dressing-stool. She should have stayed to face them both, told Charlot the truth and let Dracon do his worst in revenge. Then she could have left, not needing to care how his Leloupblanc vanity managed to explain away her rejection of him, nor that she left the field clear for Ninon Chauvet, if she were to believe Charlot's tart gossip.

But between that belated resolve and her courage to carry it out, there was the image of Elaine's sweet pale face and her contorted body, and with a sinking of her spirit Tara knew that Elaine's happiness had to be the keynote to any of her own future actions.

For Dracon, in the rare and only touch of human kindness she had glimpsed in him, had ruled it so.

*

Tara had to unlock her door to the maid who brought her early coffee. On the tray was a slender silver vase anchoring an envelope and holding a single red rose— Dracon keeping up the fiction of their engagement even in front of the servants, Tara guessed when the girl said both the note and the flower were from 'Monsieur.'

The note said curtly;

'Charlot has work to do today, so cannot keep another rendezvous in place of the one I interrupted. His regrets about this. I do not as a rule take breakfast, but Tante Mathilde and Elaine will meet you at it. *Bon appetit.* I shall be back from Bordeaux in the early evening and I shall expect you to allow me to take you out to dinner.'

So she was to be allowed all day in which to mull over his reaction to this morning's scene. Dracon certainly understood the refinements of minor torture, she thought, quite sure that Charlot had sent her no message of regret through Dracon, and suspecting the dinner-date was mere window-dressing to emphasise the 'engaged' couple's need to be alone together.

Meanwhile, all through *petit déjeuner*—the simple breakfast of coffee and rolls and honey—she had to be on her guard against revealing to Mathilde and Elaine how little she knew about Dracon's work and habits. She dared not ask how much of his time was spent at his Bordeaux offices, in order to find out how much she would have to see of him, and she had to wait for Elaine to tell her that he and Charlot did not travel into the city together. Dracon was usually driven by his chauffeur; Charlot had a small runabout for his sales itinerary. Sometimes he was away for several days at a time. 'When one could not say which of us misses him most, I or Elaine,' supplied Mathilde fondly. 'For they are so close, these two, and Charlot so protective, so gentle always—— Is he not, *chérie*?' she appealed to Elaine, who answered with a lack-lustre 'Yes,' bringing a frown to Mathilde's brow.

'You must not worry, little one. He has moods, yes, but all young men have them. And it is Dracon we should blame, for hounding him about his work. Impatient as he is with you of late, he does not love you the less. For if he were growing cold to you, I, his mother, would be the first to know it,' she assured the girl with confidence.

After breakfast she suggested that Elaine should show Tara over the house and grounds, saying that it would serve as the walking Elaine must do every day. Had Tara and Dracon made definite plans as to when he would make her mistress of the place? she wanted to know. To which Tara could only reply with the truth that they hadn't discussed any dates at all as yet.

The house was gracious and serene, its family rooms furnished for comfort and its stately ones with dignified taste. It was pleasant with present sunshine and mellowed by all the past warmth of climate it had known, and Tara was conscious of a pang of envy of whatever woman might one day be its mistress. That meant she would be Dracon's wife ... paying for her

bed and board with the same submission to his mastery
as he commanded from the others of his family. Or
was it possible that this faceless, nameless woman
might actually love and value him for what he was? Or
that he might love her as other men loved—with
friendship and tenderness and passion? But though
Tara dismissed so ludicrous a thought, her envy lingered, not now only of the house, but of whatever the
woman of her fantasy might learn and know of Dracon
which she, Tara Dryden, never would.

For instance—his touch, his arousal of the senses,
his claiming—last night, all simulated with her for
Charlot's benefit, but in love, how real, how intense,
how rapturous for both——? No, she must *not* allow
her body to remember and thrill to the false ecstasy of
it. That made her as guilty as he.

There was a rose garden in the shape of a star, and
a circular herb plot, spaced out in segments for each,
and long borders and tended lawns, a grape and peach
house, a swimming pool and stables with boxes for six
horses—Dracon's two, Charlot's and Elaine's mares
and two others.

Elaine asked, 'Do you ride?'

'Latterly, only when I go home to Ireland for a holiday. Then I hire from a livery stable,' said Tara.

'But you do? Dracon must have told you we all ride
here?' Elaine pressed.

Dracon hadn't. 'I didn't bring any riding gear,' Tara
excused herself.

'Tch! How could he have let you come without it!'

Elaine exclaimed. 'But no matter—you have slacks, and you will ride with me?'

'Don't you go out with Charlot?' Tara asked, remembering last evening's scene.

Elaine sighed. 'When he is here. But since Filoselle has been sick, he has not wanted to. That is'—she ran a hand down a silky mane—'I think it is only since then. But he has been different, sometimes ugly-tempered since he came back from England before we expected him.' She paused, then turned troubled eyes on Tara. 'Is it possible he met another girl in London and liked her better than me? Ought I to ask him about it, would you say?'

'I shouldn't, if I were you,' Tara advised. 'If he didn't want you to know, he needn't admit it. You wouldn't want him to think you don't trust him, and while he doesn't volunteer anything about another girl, you are only worrying without cause.'

Elaine admitted, 'I'm not *really* worrying—only wondering at his mood. I know he loves me. And you know about us? That we have always been sweethearts, and that we shall marry when I am stronger and when Dracon decides that Charlot can keep me? Dracon has told you? Or no——' she corrected herself—'you knew Charlot first, so he will have told you about me?'

'And about the château and all of you,' Tara confirmed in half-truth.

'How did you meet Charlot?'

'We were introduced.'

'And Dracon?'

'Through Charlot.'

Elaine pursued relentlessly, 'But why did he behave so badly when you met again yesterday? I had had to go to bed before he came in last night, and he had gone before I got up this morning.'

This was dangerous ground. Tara said, 'Perhaps Mademoiselle Chauvet was right. Didn't she suggest that he didn't approve of me for Dracon?'

'Perhaps,' Elaine nodded. 'Though it is more likely he wanted to annoy Dracon. That is, if Dracon had brought home Helen of Troy herself, Charlot might have thought it clever to try to snub them both.' She changed the subject, to Tara's relief. 'You will ride with me this evening?'

'I'm dining out with Dracon this evening,' Tara told her.

'Tomorrow, then. I have to rest through the siesta hour.' She looked at her watch. 'I had better swim now. Dracon will want to know whether I have today. You will swim too?'

'I'd love to.'

Dracon ... Dracon ... Dracon. His name ran like a dark thread through the story of these people's lives, thought Tara.

Charlot's was ordered by his disapproval, Elaine's by the timetable he expected her to keep, Mathilde's probably by her dependence on him. He had only to jerk the thread for them to answer to its twitching. As she had done herself, was doing still. Why? What claim had he upon her that she could not deny him? What more might he ask of her before she found the will to break the thread and escape?

She had always thought that when she loved she would feel happy and eager to be as beholden as this. But what held her captive to Dracon Leloupblanc? Though she had asked the question, she told herself she did not want to know.

After the noon meal the peace of siesta settled down upon the house and gardens. Tara, used to office work in the afternoons, did not need to rest, so she decided to explore further afield when a gardener, taking his ease in the shade, told her she was free to go anywhere on the estate, though she might find the paths rough and untended. 'Mademoiselle Chauvet employs no staff to keep her property in repair,' he explained.

Then why did she refuse it to Dracon? Tara wondered as she walked the parched fields, as empty of crops as their irrigation channels were choked with rubble and weeds. Here and there were derelict work-sheds, and rusty wire still fastened to drunkenly leaning stanchions probably spoke of rows of vines once supported by them. No wonder Dracon wanted to buy and turn such an eyesore into profit! Tara could imagine how it must offend his perfectionist eye as well as his pocket.

There were no hedges and she was on a narrow stony path between two such neglected vineyards when she heard a clatter of hooves coming up behind

her and she had to jump down from the path to allow
the rider to pass. But instead the big black horse
skidded to a rearing halt just where she had been
walking, and she saw that the rider was Ninon
Chauvet. She recognised the horse too as one from the
château stables.

Ninon was laughing as she leaned to pat its neck. 'I
allowed Le Garou to startle you,' she said in English.
'But no doubt you know this is my land, do you not?'

Tara did not miss the implied rebuke. 'Yes. Mons—
that is, Dracon had told me. But one of his gardeners
said you wouldn't mind if I explored it,' she replied in
French.

Ninon's pencil-thin brows lifted. 'You deceived us
all last night—you speak very good French,' she said.

Tara smiled. 'Nobody asked me whether I did or
not. And of course I want to practise it.'

'But *naturally*! Dracon will expect it in his wife.
Word-perfect, no less—— And I was not serious about
your trespass. As *châtelaine* of Isray, you will go where
you please. You have seen my house? You have walked
so far?'

When Tara said no, Ninon dismounted. 'You must
see it. But as a mere peasant-owner, I must not ride
while you walk. Go ahead, and Le Garou and I will
follow,' she urged.

Not at all sure that the banter did not hide hostility,
Tara obeyed. Over her shoulder she asked, 'Didn't I
see your horse in Dracon's stable this morning?'

'Yes. He belongs to Dracon. Myself, I call him Le

Garou for short. But his real name is Le Loup-Garou
—the He-wolf, the Wild One—and only Dracon or I
can ride him,' said Ninon. 'You ride yourself, of
course?'

Her cottage, Le Douaire, the dower-house, stood in
a dip of the land, surrounded thickly by trees which
hid it from any but a near view. Its furnishings were
rather Eastern in style, with brass tables and piled
cushions and fretted dark oak and branching cande-
labra. Watching Tara appraise it, Ninon murmured,
'You find my home a little too exotic for your taste?
But that is intentional. Here in the South people
furnish too sparsely—two upright chairs, a table, a
bureau—that is enough. But for me luxury, even a
trace of the voluptuous, is important, and men, in
certain moods, appreciate it too ... Dracon, for instance, has often said he can relax here——' She stopped to sigh. 'But that of course is in the past now—he
could relax here; he cannot again.'

Since her meaning was clear Tara did not give her
the satisfaction of asking why not, and the remark was
the first of several such arch hints that she and Dracon
had enjoyed an intimacy which his engagement to Tara
would spoil, and that she accepted her ousting from his
favour. Yet beneath the cover of her self-effacement
Tara sensed the sharp claws of hostility showing
through.

Ninon's comments and questions were pointed and
shrewd.

What a very short time Dracon had taken to decide to marry!

How would Mathilde react to Tara as the château's new mistress?

The château—a perfect setting for the wedding. Tara really must not be married from anywhere else! Except, of course, that Dracon might expect her to meet some of his late women-friends among the guests——! Ninon thrust, and Tara feinted, recognising she had made an enemy through no fault but that of Dracon's false claim upon her, from which, did Ninon know it, she had nothing to fear.

Meanwhile for Tara there loomed her tête-à-tête dinner with Dracon, there being no doubt in her mind, when he joined her and Mathilde and Elaine for the evening ritual of drinks in the courtyard, that he had made the opportunity in order to catechise and blame her for her dawn encounter with Charlot. He kissed her, apologised for having had to leave that morning 'before you would have been stirring', asked Elaine how she had spent her day and was telling Mathilde to which restaurant he proposed to take Tara when Charlot appeared.

'*Chéri!*' Elaine put out a hand to him, her eyes bright with welcome. After a moment's hesitation he slouched over to her, kissed her clumsily and went to pour himself a cognac.

'Sir!' Dracon rasped. 'Your mother! Tara!' he indicated.

Charlot shrugged and turned from the drinks table.

He nodded to Mathilde and slanted a glance at Tara. 'I'm *sorry*!' he apologised elaborately. 'Ignore your utterly dazzling fiancée—why, how could I?' he drawled before strolling back into the house.

Though Mathilde cleared her throat nervously and Elaine concentrated on twisting her fingers into a cats' cradle in her lap, his audience made no comment. Dracon looked at his watch and suggested Tara should go and dress, as he would like to show her some of the city while the evening light held.

Debating what she should wear, she was half tempted to take no trouble to do him credit. But since her original intention had been to continue to charm Charlot, she had brought nothing particularly unbecoming with her. And in any case, her feminine pride would not let her appear less than groomed for Dracon's cold, appraising eye. In a whim of nostalgia for how carefree and uncommitted she had been when she had last put it on, she chose the silver-grey jersey gown of her first meeting with him. He had affected to admire her looks then. Would he find it necessary to go through the same false motions tonight?

Driving into Bordeaux and showing her its ancient and modern sights, he could not have been more informative a guide. He described and demonstrated how the great moon-curve of the river made it the near-perfect port which it had been more modestly since the time of the Gauls, before Christ. In the production and sale of wine it was supreme, and though it owed its prosperity to trade, it was also a meeting place for all the arts of the world. His own offices were near the magnificent House of Wine, the official headquarters of the industry, the building itself on the site of an ancient vineyard.

They dined at Dubern, a restaurant where Dracon seemed to be well known and where several of his friends came over to speak to him, to each of whom he introduced Tara as his fiancée, to her embarrassment.

After the third such encounter she objected, 'You must dine here often. Is it necessary to single me out from other women guests your friends must have seen you with from time to time?'

Dracon shrugged. 'Necessary? Not strictly. But as word will get around about our engagement, I thought I might as well give them the chance to claim that they have met you personally.'

'And when the engagement comes to nothing?'

'Then they can tell everyone they could see from the beginning that we weren't suited. But its ending is a hazard we needn't discuss at this stage,' he retorted crisply. 'Meanwhile, tomorrow I must buy you a ring.'

'You can't! I won't accept it!'

'Then we will compromise. I shall give you an antique one which belonged to my mother, and you will wear it, please, while our arrangement needs to last.'

Tara did not argue. It was hopeless. He had an answer to everything. She could only be thankful that so far, except for this brush, which she had rashly invited, his manner had been no more than that of an attentive escort, bent on entertaining her. And indeed, a little heady with good wine and his gourmet's choice of food for her, she could almost persuade herself that he did not mean to take her to task over the morning's scene with Charlot. To feel relief at that was craven of her, she knew. But for some reason she didn't want this civilised evening to break up in more of the sordid conflict to which he had committed her. When they parted at the end of it, she would have liked to be able to tell him sincerely that she had enjoyed it, and there was small hope of that if, later, he chose to force her on to the defensive, as he usually could.

As he did—when she had begun to think he really had had no ulterior motive in taking her out. They were on the way back to Isray when he enquired acidly, 'Tell me, whose was the idea of the hasty rendezvous with Charlot this morning—yours or his?'

Tara said, 'Mine. I waylaid him. You may not have heard me, but I warned you last night that I meant to.'

'Breaking our agreement that, for Elaine's sake, he must be persuaded that we are engaged? You told him it wasn't true?'

'No. *No*—I'd given you my word!'

'Under pressure. But why had you to see him?'

She was glad he couldn't see the colour which she knew was flooding her cheeks. 'I couldn't bear him to think I had invited you into my room, or that— that——'

'That our goings-on were our usual nightly habit? Though, having known you himself, was he likely to believe you? In these days, engaged couples do enjoy a certain amount of licence, you know, and I had put considerable thought into making the scene convincing.'

'Charlot never did "know" me in the way I think you mean,' she denied.

'The progress of your affair with him being cut short by my rude intervention? Too bad,' Dracon mocked. 'However, were you able to persuade him of your innocence?'

'No.'

'Not even when you flung yourself into his arms, pleading with more than your lips?'

'I didn't throw myself at him. I stumbled and he had to catch me!'

'And kiss you to some purpose, I noticed.'

'I suppose he felt he had to punish me. He was angry and hurt, and if you'd heard him before that, you'd know he wasn't kissing me for love just then. And as you said your purpose behind all this—this charade was that he should hate and despise me, you seem to have succeeded already, and you can let me go.'

Had she ever hoped he would agree? When Dracon shook his head, she knew she had not. It could not be as easy as that.

'Look,' he said, confirming that it wasn't, 'you can't wriggle free that way. You may have done your best to foil me by whining to Charlot that what he saw last night was not real, but even if he believed you, which you say he didn't, that doesn't send him back to Elaine —yet.'

'You can't force him back to Elaine.'

'He should come round to it before she has despaired of having to love enough for two. But only so long as *you* are out of his thoughts, which you are not yet by a long way. His jealousy may want to hate and spurn you, but it can't. Hence the punishing kisses, instead of turning on his heel and calling it a day. He is rude to you in public, yes. But how soon is Elaine going to guess that all those sulks in your presence go a good deal deeper than mere dislike?'

'She doubted it today, but I told her it could be because he thinks I'm not good enough for you, and she seemed to accept that.'

'As if he had any right to question my choice, which he hasn't and which Elaine knows he has not,' Dracon scoffed. 'No, my dear, I am going to have to work faster, and you are going to have to try harder than you have done to date. For instance, no further collusion with Charlot, you understand?' he demanded.

'You've appealed to me for Elaine's sake, but there's no way in which I can help you more,' Tara returned bleakly.

'You can co-operate in all I see fit to do, including, if necessary, further public demonstration of my passion for you.' He paused, then went on, 'Something else you must understand—there is more to this exercise than my concern for Elaine. I have told you already that Charlot is less than useless to the firm while he is moonsick for you. When he was in London he squandered his time on you, and since he has been back at work his record has been abysmal. As he is going now, he is well on the way to becoming the feckless parasite his father was, and before that happens *I* mean to see him happy enough again with Elaine to put some kick into his work, and she, please God, without more than a passing glimmer that their affair was ever in danger.' Dracon paused again. 'You will go along with me in this?'

For the first time it was a question, not an order, evoking in Tara a reluctant respect for his sincerity.

Clearly he cared for Elaine and not less, though differently, for Charlot's future. And though he had to be wrong in thinking he could shape them—and herself —to his pattern, something within her quickened and responded to a dynamism of purpose which left him in no doubt he could order it so. *Where the wolf leads* ... in this, as always, Dracon intended his pack should follow. But this time, his asking her help instead of demanding it disarmed her will to resist.

She asked obliquely, 'Charlot's father? Your uncle, Henri Leloupblanc?'

Dracon nodded. ' "Speak only good of the dead," ' he quoted. 'But Henri deserves less charity. If my father hadn't been shrewd enough to will the firm to me, leaving Henri and Mathilde and Elaine dependent on it, Henri would have ruined it in a couple of seasons, and I am not seeing Charlot head in the same barren direction. Before he met you, I planned to groom him for executorship in time, and I still mean to, once he has been brought to his senses over Elaine.'

Tara demurred, 'He confided to me that he wasn't happy in his job.'

'So he claims now. He did his military service in the air force, and he has romantic ideas of a flying career. But he likes the money I pay him, and while he is the only male Leloupblanc in line to me, he remains within the firm. That is, at least until I have a son.'

(A son by would-be predator, Ninon Chauvet?) Aloud, Tara asked, 'And do you think it fair to make him wait on that?'

Dracon had turned in at the château gates and he swept the car to a halt in front of the house before he answered. He switched on the courtesy light and turned in his seat, his eyes narrowed upon her.

'*I* am waiting upon it until I marry,' he said unanswerably. 'Why shouldn't he?'

CHAPTER FOUR

THE next morning Tara woke again at first light and opened her windows to the dawn chorus of the birds, feeling fairly confident that even if Charlot went early to the stables, he was not likely to intrude upon her. Dracon had not reported what had passed between them yesterday morning when she had fled from them both, but that it would have been enough to ensure that Charlot would keep his distance from her she had little doubt. Dracon would have chosen his censure well, with care for every withering word . . .

On her way back to lie propped in her bed she paused by the dressing-table where lay the further 'evidence' of their engagement which he had pressed upon her before they had parted for the night. The house had been asleep when they went in, but a tray of drinks had awaited them in the hall. Dracon had poured himself a cognac; Tara had refused anything and had been about to say goodnight and leave him, when he put down his glass, said 'Wait——' and had left her.

When he came back he was carrying a velvet dress-ring box, at sight of which her heart sank. He had been serious then about giving her his mother's ring, and he was going to insist she take it—and he had.

She picked it up now—an eternity circlet of rubies set in a broad band of chased gold. He had taken it from its box and drawn it down her engagement finger, twisting it forward and back to ascertain its fit, which, as it happened, was perfect.

They had both stood looking down at it. She hadn't known what to say at a moment which should have spelt magic for her, but was utterly false. She had pulled at the ring in rejection of it, but his hand had clamped down over both of hers. 'No!' he ordered. 'You agreed to our bargain and you will wear it—our advertisement to all interested parties that we are in the total accord they expect of us.'

'It was your mother's—I wonder that you dare,' she had breathed.

He had shrugged. 'My mother was a realist,' he said. 'She would have agreed that the end justifies the means, and didn't you notice that tonight my friends' womenfolk all looked at your left hand to see if you were already wearing my ring?'

Tara hadn't answered, and she had left him then. There had been nobody there to perform to, so he had let her go without touching her, his indifference to her as cold as his show of passion had been hot. To him she was only a tool he was wielding with skill and direction—no more to their relationship than that he made use of her as he willed. Fingering the ring, admiring it for the heirloom it was, she felt a stab of regret at its lack of meaning between them. Supposing her feeling for Dracon had tempted her to welcome him dangerously in her room; supposing his desire-driven embrace of her and her willing yielding to its temptation had been real, then the gift of his ring last night would have been a real earnest of their love. However mild their parting after a happily shared evening, it would have been full of promise, and this morning she would not have been handling a mere piece of jewellery, feeling rejected and bereft (of what?) and very much alone.

She wore the ring when she went to breakfast, at which everyone but Charlot was present. Dracon drew Mathilde's attention to it, and Mathilde kissed Tara warmly, saying how glad her *belle-soeur* Drusille would have been to see Dracon's fiancée wearing it, adding wistfully that she herself had nothing so valu-

able for Charlot to give to Elaine when their engagement was official. At which Elaine claimed loyally that
she didn't care if her ring came from a chain store;
she had told Charlot so often enough.

Dracon said drily, 'When the time comes, he will
give you a diamond or explain to me why not.' Then
he softened that by telling her he had sent Charlot in
to the office early, so that he could have the afternoon
off to take her out.

Elaine glowed. 'Oh, thank you. Where?'

'Wherever you choose. Lunch somewhere on the
river, perhaps?'

'I'll let *him* choose,' she said contentedly, and was
asking Mathilde whether they need be back to dinner
when Dracon told Tara, 'Ninon Chauvet rang to say
she wants to talk business with me over a drink this
morning, so I'll take you down to the dower-house with
me, if you would care to come?'

Tara was not anxious to see more of Ninon Chauvet
than she need, but after Charlot's hints and Ninon's
claims of Dracon's intimacy, she was curious to see
them together. She supposed they would walk over
through the neglected vineyards, as she had done
yesterday, but Dracon took his car, as he would be
going on to the office afterwards.

Ninon greeted him with the conventional kiss on
each cheek, allowing her hands to slide down his arms
caressingly before she stood back.

'My *good* Dracon!' she crooned. 'So ready always to
come when I call!' She turned to include Tara in a

smile which had thinned. 'But isn't Tara going to be very bored with our business talk? Perhaps,' she offered, 'we ought to put it off to another time?'

She could hardly have made Tara less welcome, but Dracon said crisply, 'There's no need. I shouldn't have brought Tara along if she couldn't hear the details of any business of yours which also concern me.'

Ninon flashed, 'How do you know it concerns you?'

'When you call me in a panic of urgency, it usually does. What is it this time? An offer for the estate which we shall discuss at length but which you will already have made up your mind to turn down, whatever my advice?'

'Oh, Dracon,' she pouted, 'you guess too much.' She turned with a shrug to Tara. 'My best friend, as I told you yesterday. But he can be so cruel.' Busying herself with bottles and wineglasses, 'As you yourself may find one day,' she finished.

'Why should she?' Dracon asked with a lazy smile as he took his drink from her.

'Because, my friend, it is your nature to make suffer those you—care about. Whether for their good or for your own pleasure, who can tell? But that it is so, even your new fiancée will learn,' she told him with the bitter candour of one who, Tara felt, like herself, knew what it was to be at the receiving end of his ruthless dominance. But as if the note of spite behind the words had escaped him, he merely laughed outright.

'Dire warnings for a bride-to-be! Really, Ninon, you should be wearing your fortune-teller's hat instead of your business one!' he taunted her, then added more briskly, 'But to this latest offer—for I am right, you have had one?'

She nodded. 'Through my solicitors.'

'For how much?'

Ninon named a sum of so many millions of francs that Tara felt in need of a calculator to translate it into sterling. But Draçon seemed unimpressed. 'And what have you said to it?'

'It is the highest bid yet, but I told them I should consult you about it.'

'Consult me, or dangle the offer before me to see if I'll make an advance on the figure?' Dracon asked drily.

'Consult you, of course,' she pouted. 'You know I wouldn't accept anything without your approval.'

'A truly novel way of doing business!' he scoffed. 'Ask one client if you should take his rival's offer, and be prepared to turn it down if he advises against!'

'But you aren't a client for the land—with rivals. You know that,' she protested.

'And *you* know that I would take the land off you tomorrow if you would name your terms. So what does that make me but a client for it? Or is it perhaps in your mind to make me a present of it without strings?' he finished ironically.

Ninon looked away from him. 'No, I am not giving it to you. And I am not selling it either,' she said.

'Either today or tomorrow; either to me or to your latest bidder?'

'To neither of you. It isn't for sale.'

Dracon spread despairing hands. 'Then what are we talking about, *mon bijou*? You had made up your mind before you ever called me, as usual. So what was there to discuss?'

She brought her glance back to meet his. 'Don't call me your jewel in front of your fiancée—she won't like it,' she snapped. And then, when she saw he was standing and offering a hand to Tara, 'You are not going?' she pleaded. 'I know I said drinks, but I thought you would stay to lunch——'

He shook his head. 'I am sorry, no.'

'But Tara will?'

'I am sure she would like to.' Which settled the question. He left, and Tara, none too willingly, stayed.

The exchange between Dracon and Ninon had puzzled her. His manner had been that of his own caustic brand of aloofness, but what was their real relationship? she was surprised to find she wanted quite badly to know. Whatever it was, she grudged it to them ... *Grudged* it? The thought was a shock. What was it to her how long or how well they had known each other; how true were Ninon's claims that Dracon found relaxation only with her; how careless or deliberate had been the endearment for which Ninon had chided him; how true or unfounded had been Charlot's taunts that Ninon would see her 'engagement' to Dracon as a threat to her own rights in him?

It could only be, surely, her instinctive dislike of Ninon which resented their intimacy? Her jealousy of it had nothing to do with her own brittle, unsought relationship with Dracon—had it? In competition with Ninon for Dracon's attention? The very idea was absurd. And yet——

Ninon served a vegetarian highly-spiced meal which was in keeping with her other exotic tastes. Afterwards there was thick black coffee with a cloyingly sweet liqueur. Ninon's conversation was mostly personal, and at last she asked, 'I expect you wonder why I won't name a price for the estate to Dracon, don't you?'

'I rather think *he* must wonder,' Tara parried guardedly. 'But where would be the point, if you don't mean to sell?'

Ninon echoed, 'Where indeed?' She paused. 'Since I don't mean to sell it to him for money, at any price.'

'Not for money? What do you mean? I thought that, though you are turning it down, you were considering an offer you have had?' Tara puzzled.

'You misunderstand me. I said "not for money" to *Dracon*. For him I am reserving different terms. As for the other offer'—Ninon shrugged—'I merely quote it a quarter of a million francs or so higher each time.'

Tara's intuition jumped a gap. 'You're saying you called Dracon to consult him about an offer you hadn't really had?'

Ninon nodded. 'You are shocked?'

'But why? You've done it before?'

'Yes.'

Remembering Dracon's dry comments, 'But doesn't

he realise by now that the offers aren't genuine?'

'He probably does, but I name no names, and he can't prove anything. As for why—because it whets his appetite to let him think from time to time that I *might* sell over his head, if the price were high enough. Not knowing, you see, that my terms *to him* are not financial at all——' Ninon broke off to question Tara, 'And now you are asking yourself why I am confiding all this?'

Tara murmured, 'I am hoping you won't regret it. It's all very personal between Dracon and yourself.'

'But also to you, I am afraid.' There was a green glint in Ninon's eye as her glance caught Tara's and held it. 'To you,' she went on, 'as Dracon's fiancée, to whom he can't keep his promise of marriage if he marries me in order to get possession of the estate. For those are my terms to him, my *only* terms. No love, no pledging to cherish, for Dracon can't love. He can only covet and manoeuvre to get, and once you free him, giving him any reason you like, he will take marriage to me in his stride, as the saying goes, when he realises the land comes with me as my dowry.' She drew a long breath. 'There! You cannot claim I am not frank with you. What do you say?' she concluded.

The sheer audacity of the woman! Tara gathered her forces. 'More than you will welcome, I think,' she said. 'For instance, why have you waited until Dracon has pledged himself to me before issuing your ultimatum of marriage to him—or no deal?'

'Because until now—I am still frank, you see—time

has been on my side. While Dracon had no other plans for marrying, I could afford to wait, teasing him now and then with the threat that I might sell to someone else. But now he produces you as his intended bride, and my plans have to crystallise before it is too late. It is as simple as that. You see?'

That Ninon seemed to be enjoying herself Tara found so infuriating that she might have been defending a real engagement which mattered to her when she retorted, 'I should have said it was already too late when he's engaged to someone else. To expect me to give him up so that you can bargain with him on your own terms is surely asking too much?'

Ninon agreed blandly, 'It would be, and I should expect to fail if I thought he loved you more than he wants my land. For—forgive me, will you not?—I have known him better and for longer than you have. Offer him a choice between the ownership of Isray and marriage to any woman he has yet met, and I know what his answer would be. In marrying me, he wouldn't have to choose. As for love, that's a bagatelle I shouldn't ask of him, knowing I should ask in vain.'

'Then why——?'

'Because, though I own Isray, it gives me no standing. What am I? A spinster, living in a little cot the size of a *pigeonier*, whereas, as Madame Leloupblanc of the Château d'Isray, I should share Dracon's status; people would be answerable to me; I should be someone, and Dracon's ambition alone would open any door to me—any door at all! And because I want *that* of my future, I want Dracon too.'

Appalled by the cold calculation in Ninon's tone, Tara asked, 'And it wouldn't matter at all to you if I told you I love Dracon too much to give him up?'

'Matter? Why should it? I hardly know you, do I?' Ninon enquired. 'Besides, as I've told you, I wouldn't ask it, if you had any hope of his loving you. Because he doesn't and won't, you know. Being who he is, he could only have proposed to you for some ulterior motive of his own. For he doesn't love people—only power.'

How uncannily near to the truth of Dracon's motives was Ninon's guess, Tara knew only too well. But she had to meet bluff with bluff. 'And when I tell you that I haven't the slightest intention of breaking my engagement for your reasons, aren't you afraid I may go straight to Dracon and tell him what you have asked?' she said.

Ninon shook her head. 'I don't think you will.'

Tara knew she would not. But, 'Why shouldn't I?' she asked.

'Because, unless you are wilfully blind to whatever use he has for you, you must know how frail your hold on him is. So you won't run to him with the news that he has only to apply to me for Isray—and he can have it on my terms ... will you? *Not* wise policy at all— to volunteer to the man you want that you know you have a rival!' Ninon taunted. As she saw Tara was standing, about to leave, she went on, 'You are thinking that if we have to meet even once more, it will be too often? But I'm afraid I have to be around, so we must appear polite. And you needn't fear that I shall ask you again to give up Dracon to me for his own good and, did you but believe it, ultimately yours.'

Tara summoned irony to the aid of her anger. 'That's very civil of you, I'm sure,' she said.

'Isn't it? It means I shall have had to give myself the trouble of thinking of other ways of seeing you off,' returned Ninon, snatching the last word.

The utter, utter falsity of it all! thought Tara as she walked back to the château across the disputed, derelict vineyards. They stretched in every direction, dry, stony and barren, as if in mute appeal to the elements of sun and rain and the skills of men's hands to bring them to life again. Dracon could do it if he had the right, but Tara's spirit cried out in protest at Ninon's coldblooded terms. She heard herself arguing with Ninon as if she really had a prior claim to Dracon. She had even appealed in the name of the love Ninon would assume she had for him, and had surprised herself with the sincerity with which she had defended her 'engagement'. She might almost have cared for it to mean something precious to her instead of its being the dispassionate pact Dracon had made of it. If only Ninon knew it, the ring on Tara's finger spelt no danger to her plans. And yet—'Over my dead body!' Tara found herself muttering dramatically at the thought of a marriage between Dracon and Ninon, each for their self-interested ends.

It was an empty threat, she knew. For what could

she do to prevent it, once Dracon had done with her services and she had left the château? Nothing, of course, and only Ninon's belief in their engagement was keeping her at bay meanwhile. Tara wondered why she had resented more than anything Ninon's certainty that it was no love match on Dracon's part. Had Ninon touched on the raw of her pride in herself? Or on some need which could be more deeply hurt than pride—a need of something Dracon Leloupblanc hadn't, and never would have, for her? Tara had no answer to that.

Her way to the house through the gardens led past a picturesque belvedere, a little retreat from sun or rain under a stone domed roof supported by four fluted stone pillars garlanded with clematis. Within its shelter was a stone seat where, to Tara's surprise, she came upon Elaine sitting alone.

Tara greeted her, 'I thought you would still be out with Charlot. Wasn't he coming back to take you somewhere to lunch?'

Elaine said dully, 'He didn't come. He hasn't been back at all.'

Tara looked at her watch. 'But it's nearly four o'clock!'

'Yes.'

'And he hasn't telephoned?'

'No.'

'And you haven't rung the office to ask if he's been kept?'

'Tante Mathilde wanted to, but I wouldn't let her.'

Elaine bit her lip. 'I have *some* pride!'

Though Tara's instinct guessed otherwise, she objected, 'But you can't know. He may have had an accident, or be held up somewhere, out of reach of a telephone. Look, Dracon went back to the office from Ninon Chauvet's, so I'm going to ring him to see if he knows where Charlot is. What's the number?'

Elaine quoted it. 'But Charlot would have left before Dracon went back, so he won't know anything,' she added.

Nor did Dracon when, after persuading Elaine into the house, Tara asked her to stand by while she telephoned him.

His reaction was explosive. Charlot had left the office before noon. 'And you are saying that he didn't come back to take Elaine out?' Dracon demanded.

Tara said, 'He hasn't yet. She's very worried, and of course he may have had an accident.'

The sound Dracon emitted could have been a snort. 'The devil takes care of his own,' he rasped. 'He would have been carrying identification—his briefcase, samples and so on. No, time enough to ring round the hospitals when he doesn't show up tonight. And when he does——!' Leaving the implied threat in the air, Dracon paused. 'You see what this means, don't you?' he went on, then stopped again to ask, 'Is Elaine there with you now?'

'Yes.'

'Then put her on the line, will you? You and I must talk tonight,' he said, making an order of it. Tara passed the receiver to Elaine, and left her.

She came to find Tara in the garden a little later. 'Dracon is coming back early to take me riding,' she announced. 'He wants you to come with us. I told him you would object that you hadn't any riding things, but he said, as I did, that slacks and a shirt would do. Will you come?'

They were waiting at the stables when Dracon arrived half an hour later. The groom had saddled the immense Le Loup-Garou for him; Elaine's mount was a small grey called Dansette; Tara was given a mare called L'Etoile, for her white star. They rode slowly for Elaine's sake, crossing the estate to its boundaries and then taking to bridle paths through the wooded countryside beyond. Charlot was not mentioned—an ominous sign, Tara felt, of Dracon's cold wrath in store for him.

She told Dracon Ninon had been riding his mount when they had met the previous day. He asked her how she and Ninon had got on over their luncheon, and seemed satisfied with her non-committal reply. Looking across at her, he said in Elaine's hearing, 'By the way, before I left the office I rang my tailor and made an appointment for him to come out to measure you for riding clothes,'—and silenced her attempt at protest with a warning frown.

'You will be needing them,' he said. 'I blame myself for not telling you to bring some with you.'

Once, he chose to put his horse to a gallop alone, leaving the two mares to idle at a walk. As he rode away Tara could not help admiring the single, centaur-like entity he and his mount made, perfectly at one in their masculinity, their confident pride of self.

Elaine said wistfully, 'I can't think why Dracon allows Ninon Chauvet to ride Le Loup while he denies him to Charlot. He says it is because Le Loup needs more exercise than he can give him, and Charlot already has Filoselle. But Charlot is hurt and jealous, I know.'

On their return she and Tara changed and swam in the pool. They did not see Dracon again until the evening ritual in the courtyard, and they had reached the last course of dinner before Charlot appeared.

Mathilde fluttered at him, 'Oh, Charlot, why——?' And Dracon greeted him with the chilling, 'Well, sir?' of an irate parent. Elaine coloured and did not look at him. He might have been found guilty of bigamy, rather than of breaking a date, thought Tara, feeling pity and shame for them both.

Charlot ignored Dracon's question and spoke directly to Elaine.

'I'm sorry,' he told her. 'There was this fellow I'd known in the air force. He was in Bordeaux only for the day and he was alone. I took him to a café for a drink, and then I couldn't get away from him——'

'Not even to put a *jeton* in a telephone to tell Elaine you would be late collecting her?'

Dracon's voice cut across Elaine's forgiving murmur of, 'That is all right, darling. I understand,' and Charlot turned to him.

'I did ring once, but our number was engaged,' he defended himself.

'*Once?*' Dracon sneered. 'You must have been glad to be spared having to make your excuses to Elaine. Since then you will have been carousing with your boon companion, but decided you ought to show willing by turning up in time—more or less—for dinner?'

Charlot muttered, 'I don't want dinner. I've had it.'

'So? Eight hours or so with your friend, and you part over dinner?'

'No. He had to leave the city at six, but I met Ninon on the Rue Beynac and she asked me back to dinner.' Charlot turned to Elaine. 'Have you finished?' he asked. She nodded, excused herself to Mathilde, and went limping to him to take his arm.

They went out of the room together, leaving a frozen atmosphere behind them. Mathilde attempted, 'So kind of Ninon to invite him!' adding a plea to Dracon, 'One couldn't expect him to leave his friend on his own in the city, and he did try to ring Elaine——' To which Dracon replied with a short, 'If one can believe him,' and asked the maid waiting at table to bring coffee to him and Tara in the belvedere.

As he took the cup Tara poured from the silver pot the maid had brought, he commented, 'The young man is going to take some teaching, it seems. He doesn't appear to have learned much yet.'

'As if he is likely to learn anything at all from the hectoring you gave him. He is not a child, to be told how to behave to Elaine, to merit a pat on the head from you!' Tara retorted.

'And who should know better than you, from your experience of men, just how adult he is!' Dracon insinuated. 'However, that aside, why do you suppose I gave him time off, if not to encourage him to spend it with Elaine, to give their affair some new heart?'

'You expect immediate results from a few hours of freedom for him and your blessing on their picnic by the river? If I remember, you even suggested *that* to Elaine—pulling strings to make your puppets dance,' Tara scoffed.

Apparently unmoved by her vehemence, Dracon said levelly, 'I made a gesture, an opening—no more. I'd hope to have taught him—in pantomime, if you'll recall?—that you are no longer for him. You could have underlined that, if you had cared to. But of course I can't know, can I, how little you tried, or how sure of his devotion you think you can still be.'

This was unbearable. 'Are you suggesting I *want* to keep Charlot for myself? Or that I would wantonly block any way there might be of bringing him and Elaine together again? I agreed, didn't I, to go along with your cloud-cuckoo scheme?' Tara raged. 'Why did I let you bring me here, if you hadn't persuaded me that it might work?'

Dracon shook his head. 'You forget that originally you came, planning to outwit me. You meant then to increase your spell over the boy——'

'Not after I'd met Elaine, seen how she was, heard from you what she and Charlot had been to each other!'

'As you say, you were touched enough then to agree

to help me,' Dracon allowed. 'So may I take it your present tirade doesn't mean you want to go back on that? No? Good,' he approved the dumb denial of her shaken head. 'Then, unless you have something more subtle to suggest, we agree to continue and intensify the present campaign?'

'Continue for how long? And intensify how?'

'For as long as it takes——'

'That's no answer!'

'And intensify it beyond the present impasse. For instance, you could let me hear you tell Charlot in so many words that your affair is finished; that you fell heavily for me on sight.'

'Which would be a lie.'

'Or we could take our supposed engagement a stage further than I thought would be necessary.'

Apprehension shivered down Tara's spine. 'Further?' she echoed.

Dracon nodded. 'I could marry you,' he said.

CHAPTER FIVE

IF there were a telling answer to the overweening arrogance of that, Tara did not know what it was. There was outraged dignity; there was sarcasm; there was blank disbelief that the suggestion could have been made—any of which he was capable of sweeping aside. In the end she said merely, 'You seem to be able to claim a pretended engagement and be believed so far, but you couldn't fake a marriage which didn't exist.' Then, as if intending that as her only comment on a meaningless notion, she stood up, only to hear Dracon reply,

'You misunderstand me. In this case, our marriage would not only exist, but must be seen to exist. For you are so right—it would have to be proved to all interested parties.'

She stared at him. 'You're serious? You would try to go *so* far for your scheme? Give people a definite date? Make arrangements——?'

'*Mon dieu*, nothing so pretentious *before* the event. No necessity to make a public spectacle of the ceremony unless you wished it. I should be marrying you for our agreed purpose, and all we need present to our friends would be the *fait accompli*—with, of course, all the evidence of its reality which you shouldn't need me to spell out in detail.'

Tara could only gasp. 'I believe you *are* serious—but mad,' she said. 'How could you go through any such travesty without my consent?'

'Which I shouldn't get?'

'You know you would not!'

'Do I?' He came to lean against the stone pillar nearest to her, supporting himself on an elbow. 'Do I?' he repeated. 'Marriage—actual, consummated marriage—mightn't that offer you more promise in store than a pretended engagement which can be broken at any time?'

'*Promise*—in that kind of marriage?'

'Material advantage at least. After all, can you be sure of continuing success in your own profession, that you could afford to turn down a generous marriage settlement?'

She ignored the deliberate barb. 'If I were willing to tie myself down for any reason short of love, I should be as fanatically mad as—as you are.'

'Though if I went so far as to marry you in order to allow Charlot no possible hope of you, I should be tying down myself, no less than you,' Dracon pointed out.

Tara shrugged. 'That would be your problem,' she said coolly, totally unprepared for the effect the pert retort would have on him. For in a single movement he levered himself from the pillar and lunged for her, hands clamped down on her shoulders, facing her at less than arms' length.

'Every slick, trite phrase at your tongue's end——"That's your problem"; "I could only marry for love",' he mimicked her. 'How many times have you trotted out such bromides to men who may have been captivated enough by your looks and your chic to offer you marriage, instead of merely buying your merchandise? So very sure of herself, Miss English wanton! So confident she can afford to wait for her own idea of Mr Right! But what about'—he took her quivering chin in his hand, lifted it—'what about possible accident, disfiguring illness, or merely time itself which will destroy all this'—with a forefinger he traced the sculptured line of her cheek and jaw and throat—'what about when you have a lot less than you have now to attract a man, mightn't you then wish you had listened to one of them? Or even have listened to me when I suggested our marrying—for pity of Elaine?' As he finished he almost flung her from him and turned away.

Shaken and outraged, she said, 'In other words, you would ask me to buy happiness for Elaine at the expense of hope of my own?'

Over his shoulder, 'If there were no other way to ensure Charlot's going back to her, I should demand it of you in all justice,' he rasped. '*You* took Charlot from her; *you* came to Isray, pretending to agree I was right to ask you, but really meaning to charm him back again——'

'Not when I understood about Elaine!'

'But until then, to pay me out for managing my family's affairs in my own way, for its good.' He turned again to face her. 'No, I may have cheated you of some romantic dream marriage of your imagination, but I think we are all square in the matter of guilt.'

'The guilt of *another* lie? The guilt of a marriage that wouldn't *be* one?' she questioned bitterly.

His brows drew together and a cynical smile lifted the corner of his mouth. 'Are you suggesting I couldn't play the husband as well as I am acting the fiancé?'

'Oh, I've no doubt you could play it in public!' she scorned.

'Nor any doubt, I hope, that in private I should be entitled to certain rights?'

She understood him only too well. 'In that kind of marriage you wouldn't have any rights over me,' she said.

The smile became a short laugh, then vanished. 'There chants the romantic again! My dear, you delude yourself sadly if you think that in a properly witnessed and documented marriage I shouldn't both claim and take my entitlement of—shall we call her the woman in hand, however—er—part-worn she might be?'

The insult was more directly calculated than any he had flung at her yet, and Tara could only gasp in reply, remembering how impotent against him she had allowed herself to be, and remembering how once before he had thwarted her shrewish attempt to hit out at the dark, hawklike face close within reach of her hand.

Close ... closer still now as he suddenly took her into an embrace of steel-muscled arms and thrusting body which she was powerless to resist. He urged her backward until, the edge of the stone seat behind her knees, she had no choice but to sit again while he stood over her. His hands traced the contours of her breast and her torso, down over the jut of her hips and back to her waist, which they spanned, holding her captive while he bent to take his fill of experienced kisses, parting her set lips to explore the warm moistness within; sheer animal maleness seducing the senses of the female to a peak of arousal which would render her pliant, willing, giving an eager Yes to her subjugation.

As at that other time when he had pretended to make passionate love to her, Tara felt an urgency of desire which was utterly new to her. New and repugnant, because it meant she was at the mercy of her body's need to respond to a man she had every reason to hate ... who hated and despised her.

He could not beat her; he could not drag her by her hair into slavery—their common culture forbade it. But he was stating his mastery no less by this assault upon her self-esteem through this savage appeal to her sensuality, to which she must not surrender—*must not*.

He drew her to stand again. One of his hands fingered its way up her spine, the other travelled on down the swell of a thigh to her knee, where it lingered, smoothed, moved dangerously.

She tautened. 'No——!'

He released her and stood back. 'Do you expect me to apologise?' he asked.

'I doubt if you would know how. Or whether you ever do!'

'Only when I admit the need, and tonight I don't. I was only ensuring that you understood the obligations of the permanence of marriage. If it had to come to that, celibacy for either of us would be both a pity and a waste.'

'Even though——?' Tara stopped wearily. What

was the use of trying to penetrate his armour of assurance and pride of self? She put up a nervous hand to throw back her hair, which she was wearing loose tonight, and picked up her bag from the seat.

'May we go? I'm very tired,' she said, and wondered why she had asked his permission.

To her surprise he lifted the fall of her hair forward again, spreading it over her shoulders. 'Leave it,' he said. 'You look charmingly ruffled—and who would suppose we came tête-à-tête to the belvedere merely to drink coffee?'

His arm was companionably in hers as they walked back to the house.

Tara went to her room for the night when Elaine did, which, at Dracon's ruling, was always early. Under Tara's door there was a thread of light which surprised her, for when she had changed earlier she hadn't needed one. She opened and went in; Charlot was sitting near the window, the curtains of which he had closed. He stood up as she shut the room door behind her and came forward. 'What are you doing here?' she asked, dreading another emotional battle on top of the last. Besides, she needed to think ... about Dracon's demands, about the shaming thrill she had experienced at his touch, even while all her reasoning faculties were in rebellion. Marriage to him? How dared he threaten her with it? And yet——

Charlot said, 'I had to see you alone, and this was the only way.'

She went to sit on her dressing-stool, across the room from him. 'You saw me alone yesterday morning, and you refused to listen to me.'

'I didn't want to see you then. Now I do. Tara, what kind of a spell has Dracon worked on you? In London you never let me overstep a line with you, but you did let me hope,' he pleaded.

'I didn't mean to let you. I liked you, we were friends, but we had hardly had time to know each other before Dracon arrived.'

'*I* had had time enough to know I'd fallen in love with you!'

'To think you had. You'd been loving Elaine for much longer than that. For years, Dracon says.'

'And must I stay tied to Elaine, just because you jilted me for Dracon?'

'No, and I doubt if Elaine would want you "tied" to her,' Tara said quietly. 'She wants you to love her. You've been puzzling and hurting her ever since you came back from England because of your infatuation for me——'

'How dare you call it that?' Charlot flashed.

'That is all it could have been—a sudden, disastrous switch from Elaine, who's a lovely girl, and you would be a fool to let her slip away from you, when you have no possible hope of me.'

He looked at her broodingly. 'The man *has* got you where he wants you—"body and soul" as they say,' he sneered. 'And I suppose, being Dracon, he couldn't finish the job by marrying you over there? Oh no, he had to be able to flaunt you at me. "Look, my friend, she is still free to choose you if she wants to. But she doesn't. Ask her, do!"'

A thought struck Tara. Was Charlot unconsciously echoing Dracon's argument? 'Are you saying that if Dracon had brought me here married to him instead of engaged, you would have resented it less?' she asked.

Charlot shrugged. 'I don't know. Perhaps. What really revolted me was the speed with which you had gone over to him, and the way he dangled you at me as a prize that was out of my reach. Only just beyond me, if you were only engaged—a kind of torture by hope. If you had been married—oh, I don't know——' he seemed to fling the argument away from him, then asked, 'When are you going to marry, by the way?'

'We haven't arranged a date yet.'

'Well, you had better hurry. Ninon is on the warpath about you, wanting to know who you are, what you are, how you and Dracon met. She didn't invite me to dinner tonight for the sake of my beautiful eyes. She probed me for every detail I could tell her about you. For I warned you—she regards Dracon as her property that you have filched from her.'

'Yes, I know,' said Tara quietly.

Charlot looked his surprise. 'You do? How?'

'She told me so herself in so many plain words.'

'Tried to frighten you off? Too bad!' Before Tara could decide whether that was sympathy or derision, he went on, 'You said you wouldn't have accepted Dracon if you weren't sure you meant a lot to him.

TAKE THESE 4 FREE

Harlequin Romances

Thrill to romantic, aristocratic Istanbul, and the tender love story of a girl who built a barrier around her emotions in ANNE HAMPSON'S "Beyond the Sweet Waters"...a Caribbean island is the serene setting for love and conflict in ANNE MATHER'S "The Arrogant Duke"... exciting, sun-drenched California is the locale for romance and deception in VIOLET WINSPEAR'S "Cap Flamingo"... and an island near the coast of East Africa spells drama and romance for the heroine in NERINA HILLIARD'S "Teachers Must Learn."

Harlequin Romances...6 exciting novels published each month! Each month you will get to know interesting, appealing, true-to-life people... You'll be swept to distant lands you've dreamed of visiting... Intrigue, adventure, romance, and the destiny of many lives will thrill you through each Harlequin Romance novel.

Get all the latest books before they're sold out!

As a Harlequin subscriber you actually receive your personal copies of the latest Romances immediately after they come off the press, so you're sure of getting all 6 each month.

Cancel your subscription whenever you wish!

You don't have to buy any minimum number of books. Whenever you decide to stop your subscription just let us know and we'll cancel all further shipments.

Take these 4 best-selling Harlequin Romance stories FREE

... EXCITING DETAILS INSIDE

But what about you? How much does he mean to you? More than I ever did, for instance?' he added jealously.

She looked him straight in the face. 'Yes, Charlot— I'm sorry, more than you ever did,' she told him, truthfully enough. For though she had not answered the question—'Do you love him?'—which he must have thought he had asked, it was only too true that Dracon's ruthless force of character had had a unique effect upon her. From their first moment of meeting she had given more thought to him than to any other man she knew. In comparison with Charlot he towered; for Charlot there were countless parallels in other young men of his age, but when Dracon Leloupblanc had been fashioned, dynamic, utterly purposeful and ferally virile, it was as if Someone had later broken the mould ...

It was a vein of fancy which she couldn't explain to Charlot and if Dracon's plan were to succeed it was best that Charlot should continue to believe that theirs was a love match beyond any danger from him. If, when he had wanted to know what Dracon meant to her, he had really been asking, 'Do you love him?', then he must be left to think she had answered Yes.

He was standing now, preparing to go. He said heavily, 'You could live to regret it, and to wish you had let Ninon sink her claws into him instead. But that's no concern of mine, you will say.'

'No, it's not,' Tara agreed, and then appealed, 'Charlot, be good to Elaine. She doesn't know that you ever had any feeling for me, and she mustn't. But she is looking for reasons as to why you are neglecting her, and if you go on letting her down as you did today, she could guess.'

'Why, are you afraid of her hating you as much as I ought to?' he taunted.

'I'm afraid a good deal more of her having really to fear that she has lost you. So be as kind as you can, won't you? For instance, couldn't you have got away from your air force friend a lot earlier than you did, and have taken her out?'

He agreed, 'No doubt I could have, if there had been any air force friend—but there wasn't.'

'You mean——?' Tara checked in dismay.

'Just that I couldn't bear to spend a day with Elaine, thinking of you all the time. So that's what you and Dracon between you have done to her. If you don't like the result, so much the worse, and I dare either of you to blame me!' he raged.

'Charlot——!'

But either he didn't hear or he didn't mean to heed. The door of her room had closed behind him.

Tara had been frank in telling him he had no hope of her, and she had made a direct appeal to him to go back to Elaine—but had failed, she was sure. So that left Dracon's plan—with what hope of its succeeding before Elaine guessed the truth and had to face the despair from which they had hoped to save her?

How long, Tara wondered, would he expect her to pursue it before he conceded there was no future for it, allowed her to break the engagement-that-never-was, and let her go? For he couldn't force her with his even wilder threat of marriage; he couldn't marry her without her consent, and even for Elaine's sake he would not get that.

Then why, at the back of all her thought, should there be this nag of speculation as to what marriage to Dracon Leloupblanc would be like? In two false shows of pretended desire for her he had demonstrated an expertise of lovemaking which had awakened a reluctant but genuine desire in herself. But there had to be more to marriage than passion. There was friendship and respect and mutual dependence of each upon each, and a long, deep caring which would keep it sweet between the tides of ecstasy and must endure long after all the lovemaking was done.

This Tara's instinct knew beyond all doubt. Also that none of it applied between her and Dracon. But also—in a blinding flash of self-knowledge—*she desperately wanted it to*; that her resentment and rebellion was sparked by his aloofness from it, and that she would grudge his experiencing it at the hands of any other woman.

That spelled jealousy. It also spelled a need to guard him from Ninon Chauvet's coldblooded plans for him. For on Ninon's own word there would be no love between them—only for her, the social position she craved; for him, only the land he coveted and a wife who had blackmailed him into his possession of it—no less a travesty than would be his calculated marriage to Tara, should he ever seriously propose it.

If he did, what would she say? She had been so sure, and still was, that on the slim hope of their doing anything to help Elaine by their marrying, she would refuse him. But the forestalling of Ninon's icy self-interest—that was something different ... even tempting to someone who had just discovered what it was to love and the challenging need to fight on the side of the loved one, however little he recognised or cared that she was there.

She was able to sleep on the uplift of that, but day brought her down to the earth of wondering what she had been mistaking for love overnight, when only a few short hours before she had seen Dracon as her enemy, cynically regarding her as trash, but intent on using her for his own purpose. This morning, confused and bewildered, she did not know what were her true feelings towards him. Was it possible that hate and love were only the opposite faces of the same coin—both deep-felt passions, each working in turn on wavering, uncertain moods? Could she hate Dracon's heartless demands upon her, but still love and desire the man he was? The baffling truth seemed to be that she could.

Her role as Dracon's supposed fiancée was not made any easier by his suggestion to Mathilde that she ought to learn the basics of running the château. Mathilde, agreeing, was a willing and painstaking teacher; in spite of her meek subservience to Dracon's orders, she was a skilled châtelaine, able to undertake herself anything she asked of her domestics, and Tara was glad to have her time filled with watching and listening. But every time Mathilde began a piece of advice with— 'You will find that …' or told her—'Dracon manages the wine cellar himself, of course, but you will be in charge of all the household stores', Tara was stabbed with guilt at her deception of this kindly woman.

Once, while asking Tara's taste in the redecoration of a room, Mathilde broached the subject of her own future 'when you and Dracon are married'.

'If Dracon's father had been able to buy the estate when he bought the château, the dower house, where Ninon Chauvet lives, would have gone along with it, and I could have moved into that,' she said.

'But couldn't you stay here?' Tara asked. 'There would be plenty of room.'

Mathilde shook her head. 'That would not be very correct,' she objected. 'In France we elders expect to leave the family house when the younger generation marries. If Drusille, my sister-in-law, had outlived her husband, she would have moved to the dower house or somewhere similar, and that is what Charlot and Elaine and I must do—find somewhere else to live.'

'It seems very unnecessary,' Tara murmured. (As unnecessary as it's unlikely that you'll ever have to turn out for me, was her unspoken thought.) 'This house won't be any the smaller for Dracon's getting married,' she added.

'You think not? What about when you need a nursery and a playroom?' twinkled Mathilde. 'No, my dear, it is very generous of you, but leave we must. Besides, it shouldn't be long before Charlot is in a position to marry Elaine and make a home for her. By which time Dracon may have been able to persuade Ninon to sell him the estate and the dower house—leaving it free for me,' she finished with an optimism Tara wished she could share. True, given the chance she was confident she could make for herself, Ninon would 'sell' the estate to Dracon. But not for money. Only for a price which Tara knew she would dread to hear he had paid. Because that would be all she would know about it—through hearsay, after Dracon had done with her.

The summer days passed. Charlot's mare recovered, but he made every excuse for not riding regularly with Elaine. He frequently missed meals and went on sales trips which kept him away for two or three days at a time. He also often visited the dower house—a new habit, according to Elaine, who confided perplexedly in Tara, 'He always said he didn't like Ninon, but when I ask him why he sees so much of her he says she is putting business in his way, giving him introductions to sales outlets where he has had no connections until now. Ninon knows a lot of wine buyers, you see, so I suppose it could be true.'

'If he says so, I'm sure it is,' Tara comforted. 'And you should be glad if he's getting sales through her, because that will please Dracon.'

'Who never seems satisfied with the sales figures Charlot turns in,' sighed Elaine. 'And he won't let us get married until Charlot is doing what Dracon calls "proving his worth to the firm", without letting him know when that will be.'

Tara murmured, 'I'm afraid Dracon is a perfectionist, and they don't always know that a few words of encouragement work wonders where blame doesn't. But you do realise, don't you, that he is only pushing Charlot because he wants the best for you?'

Elaine turned away. 'I wish I could think *Charlot* still wanted the best for me. Or anything at all *of* me,' she said with a pitiful break in her voice.

Tara had her own ideas as to one reason for Ninon's sudden cultivation of Charlot's company. Direct appeal having failed, she had threatened to seek other ways of ridding herself of Tara, and she might have sought a ready ally in Charlot. Charlot might even have confided his own involvement to Ninon, but Tara doubted whether his pride would admit to his having been outrivalled by Dracon. No, Ninon must have other plans in which she thought Charlot might help her, but at what they could be, Tara could not guess.

She was to learn only too soon.

She was walking a path on the estate when, as once before, Ninon overtook her, riding Dracon's big stallion again. But this time Ninon did not dismount with a show of deference, and Tara stepped down from the path, prepared to wait to allow her to ride on. Instead Ninon reined-in and looked down at Tara from the advantage of her superior height in the saddle. Her mount snickered and pawed the stony path. She quieted him, '*Tais-toi, mon brave!* Tara and I must enjoy a little gossip. No chance to be private up at the house, and for some reason she does not visit me in mine any more.'

Tara said coldly, 'Can you wonder? Considering that you have made no secret of wanting to take my fiancé from me?'

Ninon conceded, 'Perhaps not, though I thought it best to be frank about my better chances with him, and I'd have expected you to see the advantage of not making an enemy of me. Because of all I know about you, I mean. For instance, would you really care for Dracon to learn that when you and Charlot first met, you weren't introduced by friends, but that you were *supplied* to him—for a price?'

Tara caught her breath, but, 'Dracon knows already how Charlot and I met,' she said with truth.

For a moment Ninon seemed taken aback. But she rallied, with a bright, 'Really? How very broadminded —and how unlike him!—to take any interest in a woman of your professional kind. You surprise me, you do indeed!'

Tara saw her opening and took it. 'Do I?' she asked, pseudo-mildly. 'Even though he must meet quite a number of us from time to time, there being, in business circles, rather a lot of us about?'

Ninon snorted, 'Oh, quite. Nowadays you are everywhere, as one knows. Not to mention your enthusiastic amateur sisters too.'

Tara hadn't finished with her. 'And men *have* been

known to engage themselves to their secretaries, or to other people's secretaries, after all,' she added with a bland smile, enjoying Ninon's blank stare before she recovered ground.

'Oh—yes,' Ninon allowed. 'Charlot did say you doubled up on both jobs, I remember.'

'He could have told you nothing of the sort!'

'Then I must have misheard him, and I'd always thought my hearing was sharp. What is more, I am quite sure he told me that before you had even met he had already paid for your services. Isn't that so?'

Tara scorned to deny it. 'Yes, he had,' she said.

'Ah! And Dracon too?'

Better to leave Ninon puzzled than to stoop to explanations, thought Tara. Summoning a falsely sweet smile, 'No, Dracon didn't buy them. To him they were free on sight,' she said, and because she would not walk ahead of Ninon mounted, or ask her to ride on, she turned back by the way she had come.

She was seething with anger, not against Charlot's 'information laid' about her but against Ninon's malicious twisting of whatever gossip she had wormed from him. Tara had felt driven to confuse Ninon with half-truths and innuendoes. But had she been wise? Or had she embroiled herself still further in matters which were none of her choosing?

That week provided ideal weather conditions for the setting of the vine blossoms. First there were some zephyr breezes to aid pollination, then some days of steady gentle rain to be followed by cloudless sunshine, during which, all over the region, the tiny hard green pellets at the heart of each flower became the promise of the wine-grape harvest to come.

All the local vineyards which neighboured the Château d'Isray were rich in verdure, showing up in sad contrast the derelict state of the château's land. Tara wondered how long Dracon would tolerate its abandonment by Ninon; remembered his assured confidence that he could win it if he tried, and asked herself whether perhaps he knew of Ninon's terms, whether neither was more coldblooded than the other and he meant to make possession of the land *his* price for marrying Ninon. In which case, they had no problem. Both would have achieved their ambitions through a calculated move masquerading as marriage, to be honoured for its face value only as far as it suited either. No more real, in fact, than the one with which Dracon was threatening Tara herself. And yet not quite the same ... For in that marriage—if it ever happened, which it wouldn't—there would be one who would have married for no advantage to herself, but only for a tangle of motives, not the least of which would have been her will to love.

The incidence of the vines' blossoming was the signal for celebration in the region. Traditionally the owners of each estate entertained their workers to a Wine Supper, and at the château it was the occasion for Dracon to give a big dinner party for his business clients and their wives.

It was so important an affair, Mathilde stressed, that it had to be catered for professionally, not only in the matter of the menu, but also in the waiter service, the flowers and the after-dinner music by an orchestra from Bordeaux.

'This year Dracon will want to introduce you as his fiancée,' Mathilde told Tara. 'It would be nice, too, if you have agreed on a date for your wedding, if he could announce that as well.'

'We haven't discussed that yet,' Tara evaded.

'But you will agree to be married from here?' Mathilde echoed her first happy acceptance of the engagement, envisaging, Tara guessed, an elaborate ceremony suited to Dracon's status, which was never likely to happen.

A week before the dinner party Dracon had told Tara that he had opened an account of twenty thousand francs for her at a Bordeaux bank. When she had protested that she would not use it, he had said, 'I expect you to do me credit in the matter of clothes, so you will use it to pay cash for anything you need, or you will have all your accounts sent to me. Take your choice.'

She had chosen neither, but had spent her own money on a new dress for the dinner party. She knew that a rich jewel-green was the perfect complement to her russet hair, which she arranged in a swathe across the back of her head, fastening it at ear level with a Spanish comb and bringing its length forward over her shoulder. Her dress was of velvet with a princess line emphasising the upward thrust of young breasts; the décolletage was draped low, the sleeves long and fitted. Narrowly strapped sandals of green and silver completed the ensemble in which she went to meet Dracon in the *salon* before his guests began to arrive.

She could see that her appearance had his approval. But it was the approval of a connoisseur, not of a lover. He said, 'You certainly make the best use of an experience which has taught you how to dress for glamour and seduction. In fact, you are so radiant tonight that, as far as beauty goes, I shall be so much the envy of my friends that I could almost persuade myself you are really my willing newly affianced bride.'

His praise had sent a glow of gratification along her nerves. 'That should make it easier for you to keep up the pretence,' she said.

'Not that it has presented much difficulty so far.'

'You are lucky. Personally I've always found that lying leaves a nasty taste in the mouth,' she retorted, not knowing why, when every impulse of her body was a-quiver to his magnetism, her tongue should be so ready with bitterness against him.

His guests included château owners from all over the region, wine-buyers, senior members of his own staff and a few of his competitors. It seemed the party was an accepted occasion for brilliance of dress and jewellery and of lively conversation, and Tara, seated beside Dracon after a bewilderment of introductions and congratulations, thought how much she could have enjoyed it all, had she been part of it by right, instead of by imposture.

The long table glittered with crystal and silver; talk and laughter and badinage went back and forth in waves of good humour; Mathilde, escorted by her son, was at the other end of the table; Elaine, at her frail prettiest, had the gallant attention of the two silver-haired 'oldies'—a Count and a Légionnaire d'Honneur —on her either side. Ninon, clothed from neck to ankle in scarlet satin with a gold-lined shoulder cape, was sitting too near to Tara for either to be able completely to ignore the other. But both managed a subtle bypassing, which Tara hoped was not too evident to their neighbours.

It was not until later in the evening that their paths crossed disastrously.

The women had left the men to their cognacs and cigars and were being served with coffee where they chose, either in the courtyard or in the house. Tara took hers with the wife and daughter of a colleague of Dracon's and with Elaine. At about ten o'clock Elaine began to look tired and admitted she was, and Tara went to her room with her. When Tara had seen her into bed they talked 'party' for a while. Elaine said patiently of her separation from Charlot, 'Of course it was right for him to take Tante Mathilde in to dinner.' And by describing them to her, Tara learned who were some of the guests whose names had escaped her on introduction.

On her way back to the party she had to pass Mathilde's suite on the first floor. Her bedroom was acting as the women guests' cloakroom; the door to it stood open and Tara was about to go in to check on her make-up, when she saw that the dressing-table was occupied by Ninon and a middle-aged woman who Tara now knew to be an American, a Madame Fahier, a wealthy widow who had been the lively centre of attention of her neighbours at dinner.

Neither woman turned as Tara, on the threshold, stepped back quickly, though not out of earshot of their voices. Nor did she move on, but flattened herself against the wall at the sound of her own name, Ninon's laugh and Madame Fahier's laconic question, 'How do you know?'

Eavesdropping was mischievous, Tara knew, but she excused it in herself when Ninon replied, 'From Charlot himself.'

'Saying he bought her services before Dracon did?'

'Ah—her Madame or her protector would have made Charlot pay. But, according to her, she offered them free to Dracon. Seeing the advantage to herself in his thinking she was generous with her favours, perhaps.'

' "According to her", you say? Then you have taxed her with it?' asked Madame Fahier.

'As soon as Charlot had told me.'

'And when you accused her of being a *cocotte*, she admitted it?'

'She had to. I had only to get Charlot to confirm it, as she knew.'

'But why your interest, my dear?'

'*Why?*' Ninon sounded affronted. 'Why, surely because we can't welcome the idea of a former call-girl as châtelaine of Isray, can we?'

Madame Fahier laughed. 'Oh, come, Ninon!' she
mocked. 'Who around here is going to mind, if Dracon
himself doesn't? Or did he engage himself to her, not
knowing this about her?'

'Oh, knowing it, since he took her on from Charlot.'

'Then, as I have asked, why your interest? Why try
to work up a scandal out of what is a commonplace in
these days?—film stars' irregular affairs and love-
nests shock no one, and a *demi-mondaine*, introduced
to us by the Wolf himself, and as charming as Tara
Dryden, can only add a touch of piquancy to life in the
region. No indeed,' Madame Fahier shook her sophisti-
cated head, 'if Dracon has accepted her and is flaunting
her with pride, you would be very unwise to scarify
the locals about her past. For your own sake, don't do
it, my girl, don't do it, I beg!'

Ninon's face, reflected in the mirror, took on a de-
flated expression. 'You don't mean you will be willing
to *know* her after Dracon marries her, if he does?' she
pouted.

'Know her? But of course! She is a poppet, as pretty
as a picture, and we are all going to *love* her!' Madame
Fahier declared gaily as she flicked exaggerated eye-
lashes with a practised forefinger and stood, brushing
herself down.

Tara escaped into the shadows of the corridor,
heartened by Ninon's defeat.

CHAPTER SIX

BUT that petty triumph over Ninon was a poor match for Tara's realisation that her departure, when it happened, would leave the field open for Ninon's designs upon Dracon—a blackmail of him which should *not* succeed if she could help it. But how could she?

She could not have said just when the knowledge flashed that the one way by which to foil Ninon's plans would be to say 'Yes' to Dracon's proposal of a bogus marriage . . . if he were serious, which of course he was not.

All the same, a decision, utterly alien, not to be considered a day or two ago, was there in her mind as a possibility, if Dracon gave her the chance to make it, and to convince him her change of heart had its private reasons.

Meanwhile Elaine drooped visibly under Charlot's neglect of her. She walked and rode and swam and rested with puppet-like obedience, but she brought no spirit to anything, making it increasingly hard to assure her that Charlot had not cooled towards her.

For only too obviously he was avoiding her, alone or in company, never now taking her on long day's sales trips, nor bringing her modest little gifts after he had been away from home; her bureau-top was a veritable zoo of toy soft animals he had brought her. But he had added nothing to her collection since he had been to England. And when she told Tara plaintively, 'That was when it all began—the change in him,' Tara had neither heart nor hypocrisy enough to urge that she was mistaken.

Had Elaine been whole and active, Tara would have advised her to cut her losses and to call upon her pride to help her to break free of her hopes of Charlot. But Elaine was too tied by the disciplines of her slow convalescence to be able to leave home or take an absorbing job. The brave resources of any other jilted girl were not for her, which made Tara's own sense of guilt the greater—as of course Dracon had reckoned upon when he had forced his misguided plan upon her.

She had known it couldn't succeed in curing Charlot of his obsession with her. How long was it going to be before Dracon knew it too? Elaine's wretchedness was surely evidence enough.

But Dracon had made no move towards conceding defeat before Ninon showed her hand again, this time directly to Tara herself.

As with Dracon's stallion, Ninon also had the freedom of the château swimming-pool. Usually Tara managed to avoid her there, but one Sunday when Dracon had been swimming too before going to change for lunch, and Tara had lingered to sunbathe, Ninon arrived. Their nods to each other were perfunctory, but when Tara began to collect her things, Ninon issued a sharp, 'Don't go. I have something to say to you.'

Tara paused. 'Something that matters?' she asked.

Ninon shrugged. 'I imagine you will think so, when you hear what it is—that people are beginning to talk.'

'About?' Tara invited.

'What do you suppose? That before Dracon took you up, you had this paid affair with Charlot which you admitted to me.'

'But how do "people" know anything about it—or think they do?' Tara asked unnecessarily.

'How? I've made it my business to see that they do. I did warn you that if you didn't get out of my way, I'd find some means of driving you out.'

'By inventing and spreading a scandal which involves Dracon as well as me?'

'I didn't invent it! I had it from Charlot and from yourself.'

'You think you had. But if I told you I deliberately misled you and denied it now, you wouldn't believe me, so why should I bother?'

'Why indeed?' Ninon echoed. 'You would be wasting your breath.'

'Though even if the story spread widely enough to hound me to break my engagement, wouldn't you have to worry about what it could do to Dracon?' asked Tara.

'Pff! It will do no harm to Dracon's reputation. *Everyone* knows that a man like him on a business trip will make use of a *cocotte* while he is away, and if he is lucky enough to get out of an entanglement which she must have blackmailed him into, so much greater the sympathy of his friends. Oh no,' Ninon forecast confidently, 'Dracon won't have to live down any scandalous story, once he is rid of you.'

'And you aren't afraid of the consequences if he ever learned that the story began with you?'

'Afraid he won't marry me, once you are out of the way and I offer him his reward? Not really,' Ninon drawled. 'Besides, if he proves stubborn, there is something else I have in my sleeve, as they say.' She slanted a look of enquiry at Tara. 'Would you care to know what it is?'

'You wouldn't have mentioned it if you didn't mean to tell me,' Tara said coldly.

'No. Shrewd of you. Well, how is this for something Dracon *won't* want known—for Mathilde's sake? That Henri Leloupblanc was my lover, for years— almost ever since Dracon's father bought the château until Henri died. Right under all their noses. How about that?' Ninon boasted.

For a moment Tara was shocked into silence. Then, 'Henri Leloupblanc? Mathilde's husband? But he was —old!' she exclaimed.

Ninon's small laugh had an ugly note. 'But not so old that he couldn't enjoy a woman who wasn't, and still is not, one hopes, exactly a hag,' she chuckled. 'Nor had he any delicate scruples about borrowing from a woman the money he needed for drink and hadn't the wit to earn for himself. No, *not* a good husband to poor Mathilde. Nor a worthy member of the proud Leloupblanc pack. But a very handy weapon against them, against Dracon, now. And don't think I shan't use it if I have to, for I *will*.'

As she spoke she stepped to the edge of the pool and dipped a tentative toe in the water. To her back Tara ground out in bitter disgust, 'You're evil! Do you know that? Quite evil.'

Ninon looked round over her shoulder. 'Yes, I know it,' she said—and dived.

There was trouble at the lunch table when Charlot, taking his place, told Mathilde he had time only for one course or he would be late for a fishing date with some friends.

Mathilde began in reply, 'If you had said so, you could have eaten earlier——' but checked at Elaine's startled cry of dismay.

'What——?' Dracon questioned as they all looked at her, staring in blank accusation at Charlot. '*Fishing*?' she echoed. 'But you can't! We are going out, you and I. Into the Landes Forest for a picnic. I have already packed our hamper!'

Charlot stirred uncomfortably in his chair. 'That wasn't for today,' he denied.

'It *was*! For this Sunday. You promised. I asked you if we could, and you said——'

Charlot admitted, 'I remember you suggested it, but all I said was Perhaps. Some time. How could I have agreed to today, when I had this date with the fellows?'

'You did, you did agree! I said Sunday, and you couldn't have misunderstood me.' Her voice breaking, near to tears, Elaine turned to Dracon. 'He is only saying this because he doesn't *want* to take me out. He never does now—never!'

Dracon said tautly, 'That has been evident for some time.' As Elaine uttered a despairing, 'Oh——' he turned to Charlot. 'Did you or did you not arrange to take Elaine into the Forest today?'

Sullenly, 'There was nothing definite.'

'She says there was, and I believe her.'

'You would—against me!' Charlot had sprung from his chair. His knuckles showed white as he clutched the back of it. 'I tell you I won't take her out. And what are you going to do about that?'

Dracon said levelly, 'I am doing nothing. *You* are. Who are these *types* you claim are expecting you for fishing?'

Charlot named them.

'Then you will ring one of them, or all of them, that you got your dates mixed and you won't be going.'

'I'll do nothing of the sort,' Charlot rebelled furiously. 'You can't make me, and if you were thinking of forcing me to go out with Elaine, just figure to yourself, will you, the kind of merry picnic we should have together—after this!' With which he flung out of the room and out of the house, as the heavy slamming of the front door indicated.

Elaine was weeping forlornly. Mathilde left her place and went to her, held her close. '*Chérie*, he did not mean to be cruel. It is only a passing storm. Perhaps he really did forget he had promised you——'

'He didn't forget. He never meant to take me. He hates me now, and I don't know why.' Elaine's voice came muffled against Mathilde's bosom as Dracon's came forcefully, 'Of course he didn't forget. In fact, one doubts if he ever had any other arrangements. But that is enough of concern with him now. I'll deal with him later. So, Mathilde, shall we go on with the meal?' To Elaine he added more gently, 'Will you stay too? Or leave, if you would rather?' and when she nodded dumb agreement with that, he went with her to the door, an arm solicitously across her shoulders.

Mathilde resumed her seat. They finished their soup in silence, and she rang for the maid to bring in the entrée. Presently she ventured, 'Charlot was right, you know. To force him into keeping his promise to Elaine wouldn't have done anything for her.' To which Dracon replied coldly,

'Do you mind, Mathilde? There is no reason at all why our meal should be disturbed further by discussion of Charlot's devious behaviour towards Elaine. Tell me, have the Quirons confirmed that they expect us to dine on Friday?'

It was a deliberate switch of subject, and they talked of other things until Mathilde decided to take a portion of the dessert, a fluffy lemon sorbet, to Elaine. When she had gone, Dracon said abruptly, à propos nothing which had gone before, 'It isn't working,' and Tara, knowing what he meant, replied, 'No. But did you ever expect it would?'

He shrugged. 'It had the best chance I could see at

the time.' He indicated her plate. 'Finish your ice, and come with me into the garden. We have to talk.'

In the garden he moved chairs under the spread of a cedar and sat facing her. Holding her glance with the hard glitter of his eyes, he said, 'So—if you have any more ways of saying "I told you so," please indulge them, and then listen to me.'

Tara said quietly, 'I'm listening. And I only agreed with you that Charlot has learned nothing from your scheme to persuade him back to Elaine.'

'Principally to convince him that he had no hope of you, trusting the rest would follow. As it might have done with your full co-operation, which I am not satisfied I have had. For instance, I have yet to see you snub him roundly. You waylaid him to explain away our tableau in your room, and what was he doing there himself the other night?'

Off guard, Tara faltered, 'He—— How do you know he was?'

'I saw him go in when I knew you weren't there. But he was early at a rendezvous, perhaps?'

'He was *not*! I found him there when I went to bed.'

'And what did he want? Or need I ask—considering that he is obviously not cured of you yet?'

Tara confirmed dully, 'You needn't ask. But he didn't get it. He pleaded with me and raged with jealousy of you, and wouldn't listen when I begged him to be as kind as he could to Elaine. And——'

'And——?' Dracon prompted her pause.

'And he still believed enough in our engagement to

warn me against marrying you.'

'With what jealous fears for you if you did?'

'I suppose—that you would treat me as you do most people, with not very much regard for any of their inclinations which clash with your plans for them.'

'H'm—much more likely that his jealousy is a good deal more earthy. Namely, that he has to admit the superiority of my sexual experience in dealing with a woman of yours. And he doesn't care for the comparison.'

'Charlot doesn't know anything about what experience I have, or have not!' Tara denied hotly.

'Then he shouldn't aspire to marriage with you himself without some idea of the intensity of courtship you'd expect of him. Or——' Dracon corrected himself smoothly, 'am I wrong, and if I gave him the green light, you and he would only need to go on from where you left off?'

Again that diabolical urge of his to goad her! Not trusting herself to reply, she asked instead,

'You said we had to talk. What about?'

'About the failure of our plan. About the alternative one I put to you, which mustn't fail. You will remember it, no doubt—a marriage which has to be the conclusive argument to Charlot's aspirations which a mere engagement wasn't?'

So he had been serious, and he meant to have her answer! She said, 'Yes, I remember. And *you* will remember that I refused?'

'Though without the moral right to refuse, considering your responsibility for Elaine's despair.'

'Which I don't admit. Nor that I could help her any more by marrying you than I have done by pretending we are engaged.'

'Showing that you underrate my ability to convince Charlot that my wife will be irrevocably the forbidden fruit which my fiancée could not be while you have been free to choose between us. When you are not free —when you have chosen marriage to me, he must realise he has no hope. After that, sanity must follow.' Dracon's gesture of spread hands was his proof of a problem solved to his satisfaction, and Tara marvelled at a blind purpose which could demand so much, having no doubt that it would be justified by results.

But he had given her the chance she had thought was beyond her reach, of thwarting Ninon Chauvet's scheming against him. He had presented her with an opening for a purpose of her own which must succeed by the very fact of their exchange of the marriage vows by which Ninon would be foiled. And so, reckless of the future she was inviting, she said, 'If you think it necessary that we marry, I am willing.'

It was typical of his confidence in his power, she thought, that he showed no surprise at what must have sounded like an incredible change of heart on her part. As if they had agreed on a deal as impersonal as a business merger, he merely said, 'Thank you. I'm glad I haven't to work at persuading you that my reasons for forcing the issue are valid, and that our marriage is the only cast-iron solution which offers itself.' He paused to look her over searchingly. 'May I congratulate you on a more graceful surrender than I thought I could hope for?'

That was too much for her pride. 'It's not a surrender; nothing so meek, I assure you,' she contradicted. 'It's merely an—an acceptance of facts.' *Facts which I know and you don't* was her unspoken thought which followed.

'Much the same thing,' Dracon replied, unmoved. 'In deciding on our marriage, I am having to accept them myself. Or doesn't it occur to you that I am not much less a victim of our circumstances than you are?'

She said, 'I think you meant it to occur to me when you pointed out that if we married, you would be just as tied down as I should be.'

'Exactly—no random exursions for either goose or gander. But perhaps I do have the slight edge of advantage over you, in that even a marriage of convenience of this bizarre sort could have its natural and desirable outcome for me.'

'Such as?' She felt herself tensed for his reply.

'Surely? It could get me a son,' he said.

Later Tara could hardly remember how from there they had gone on to discuss the coldly rational details of their commitment to each other—whether or not to announce their intention, when to carry it out and in what manner.

Dracon had asked if she preferred marriage by special licence, a civil one at the Mairie, or a church ceremony, followed by the civil one obligatory in France. She had opted for whatever would arouse the least local interest, and though he had demurred that Mathilde would be disappointed of a display, he had agreed to no announcement, no invitations and no show, prior to a civil ceremony in Bordeaux.

They had debated a date and a time and had arranged both. Dracon would tell Mathilde that he was taking Tara to Paris for a few days' shopping. They would be married at the Mairie in Bordeaux, travel to Paris for the short stay which they would make their honeymoon, and announce their news when they returned to the château. Dracon had shopped for their wedding rings without asking Tara to accompany him. He had also done some other shopping, as she was to learn, to her intense shock.

A few days before they were to leave a parcel under the label of a top couturier was delivered for her at the château. She opened the big box to find that it contained, beneath layers of tissue, three complete sets of matching satin lingerie—briefs, bras, slips, nightgowns and negligés, each set of so fine a texture that it had practically no bulk at all.

She shook out the luxurious fall of one of the nightgowns and held it against her before her mirror. From Dracon, of course. Who else would have sent her anything so intimate—and so shaming? The lovely gift made a mockery of all that a wedding present, sent in love and promise, should have meant. *This* had been as coldly calculated as had been everything about their contract; the very seductive touch and sheen of the rich material was a false witness to a false pairing which lacked any of the true reasons for marriage. And there was worse to come when she found Dracon's accompanying note.

She had just slit the envelope when there was a knock at her door. With it in her hand she went to open, to find Dracon outside.

'May I come in?' Formal, distant. She wondered if he recalled, as she was doing, the night he had entered, uninvited, and had playacted an assault which had betrayed her senses to an awareness of his magnetism which had lasted and deepened against her will. If so, he was probably enjoying the irony of his correct approach now ...

She stood aside for him. He nodded at the letter she held. 'You have read it? And you understand?'

She shook her head. 'I haven't read it yet.'

'Then please do. I expect your agreement to what it asks.'

She unfolded it and read, cold anger mounting as she did so. He had written:

'These trifles as a tribute to a chic which has all my admiration. They can be supplemented by any others to your choice. But I make the condition that all similar models in your wardrobe be destroyed before our marriage. My reason being that I am fastidious enough to be offended by other men's probable familiarity with some of them in the course

of your professional duty, I hope very much that you
will comply.'

The signature was an illegible scrawl she knew.

She crumpled the paper into her palm, in almost
the same moment of thought blaming her folly in
allowing him to continue to believe she was a woman
with a price on her favours, and resolving against dis-
illusioning him—yet.

She could do it in a sentence of four words. She
could utter them and see him crestfallen and abject
with apology—if he believed her, and he might not.
Therefore, secure in the knowledge that in the near
future which he had thrust upon her there should be a
circumstance which would force him to believe her, she
held back the words. Presently there would be a time
and a place in which they need not be spoken . . .

In the meantime she must rake his absurd conditions with all the scorn at her command. She looked
across at him. 'This is ridiculous,' she said. 'How can
you expect me to scrap everything else of this sort that
I own?'

'I do expect it,' he said. 'I have told you why.'

'At your whim of an idea that you would be at risk
of touching pitch if I decided to disobey you?' She
paused, seeking an argument, and found one. 'Don't
tell me, please, that you haven't consorted with various
women who might well have had other lovers before
you—without your being contaminated, as you seem to
fear?' she scorned.

He showed no sign of provocation. He even nodded agreement. 'Obviously you are a realist. But then, knowing men as you do, naturally you would be,' he remarked. 'However, though I admit to having indulged in other affairs with women of experience, the difference happens to be that I didn't marry any of them. I am marrying you.'

'Though thinking no better of me than you may have done of some of them,' Tara muttered. 'I don't deceive myself that you're paying me any homage by marrying me, instead of someone less useful to you than I am.'

'As I've said, a realist to your graceful fingertips,' he repeated. 'Wise of you to expect nothing not written into our contract, which, as I recall, a sentiment like "homage" isn't.'

'No. Any more than is the kind of choosy fine feeling which dictates I'm to wear clothes untouched by anyone but you. Why, reading this'—her fingers tightened on his letter—'and not knowing you haven't a shred of ordinary weakness in you, one could almost believe you were—were *jealous* of any life I've had or any men I've known before you!' she flung wildly at him.

'Think me jealous? Could one?' He appeared to consider the possibility before discarding it. 'No, if I were ever guilty of an emotion as wastefully negative as jealousy, I should do something constructive about it, believe me.'

'Constructive—such as?' she taunted.

'By asserting a claim which couldn't be misunderstood, and making it too strong to be denied,' he re-

torted crisply. 'Meanwhile,' on his way to the door he
turned back, 'will you see to the task I've asked of you,
or shall I send one of the maids to do it for you?'

Tara compressed her lips, not trusting herself to
reply. When he had gone she took out her near-
hysterical anger by shredding and re-shredding his
letter until her fingers ached.

Tara wondered how she was going to pretend to any
equable relations with him after that. But she had
reckoned without his ability to convince anyone of
whatever he wanted to be assumed about their rapport.
During the days before their 'shopping trip' he could
not have played his part better—attentive and protective of her to a degree to which she couldn't help but
appear to respond. In fact, response to Dracon Leloupblanc at his most positive was not difficult, as she
guessed she was not the only woman in his life to have
discovered. His very arrogance had a charisma of its
own.

On the eve of her wedding day Dracon's goodnight
kiss was light and tender. She slept fitfully through the
night and woke to a cold apprehension of the day
ahead. By evening she would be Madame Leloupblanc
in name, and at first waking she had to ask of her dazed
depression—*Why?*—before she remembered their two
purposes, Dracon's and her own. His, his conviction
that their marriage would act like a miracle on Charlot's infatuation; hers, her determination to foil Ninon
Chauvet's designs on him. Had there ever been any

more off-beam 'convenience' reasons? she wondered. Or at its face value, any more unworthy than her own? To use the sacredness of marriage for the defeat of another woman, however evil, had no merit in it. Only her deeper, fearfully admitted reason—that she loved Dracon—could redeem her action, and she must hold fast to that, if she were not to go back on her word. He could hurt her, taunt her to self-defensive anger, but that—to be utterly vulnerable to the other's sword-thrusts—was all a part of loving, wasn't it? And very soon now—before tomorrow perhaps?—he might not want to hurt her so much ...

She had toyed with the idea of disobeying his high-handed order to her and she had taken no steps to discarding her own lingerie. But when she dressed she wore the daytime items of his gift and packed the nightwear in her luggage. She had shopped alone in Bordeaux for her wedding suit of french blue linen with a white-veiled matching pillbox hat—gear which had to appear to Mathilde and Elaine as suitable travel wear to Paris, whatever it meant to her as Dracon's bride.

Dracon's bride! There was little in the businesslike Town Hall ceremony, witnessed by two strangers, to make her feel like a bride. The Mayor's officer's good wishes were kind but perfunctory, and her new signature in the register looked no more real than someone's experiment in trying out a new pen. They emerged from the building into a knot of reporters hopeful of some wedding news items; at sight of Dracon there was a surge round the taxi taking him and Tara to the station to catch the Paris-Sud express; flash bulbs barked, and Dracon commented drily, 'I was recognised, it seems. Which means that our news will have gone ahead of us before we get back—do you mind?'

'You mean that Mathilde and—and the others (thinking of Ninon) will have heard?' Tara asked.

'More than probably. But no bad thing, I'd say. It will save us a theatrical entrance and will have given them time to get used to the idea,' he said.

He had booked a suite in the luxury of the world-famous Georges Cinq off the Champs-Elysées; wondering what kind of a wedding night Dracon envisaged after the stark formality of their wedding, Tara noted, half in relief, half in disappointment, that the suite had two bedrooms, but at least, if he chose to ignore or reject her, she would be spared the indignity of sharing a room and a bed with a man for whom she was merely a means to an end, no more.

CHAPTER SEVEN

THEY had arrived in Paris in time for dinner. Afterwards they walked the length of Elysées in the warm night and sat on a café terrace, drinking liqueurs and coffee and watching the strolling crowds.

They talked—for one of very few times, as friends

without the menace of a sword ready to be drawn on either side. But that, Tara thought mistrustfully, was only because they avoided the dangerous subjects. Meanwhile Dracon was interesting about his work and his ambitions for the firm. She managed to draw him out about his boyhood a little, and wished he showed some curiosity about her own child and girlhood. But he did not, giving her the rather chilling impression that, as a person, she had begun for him only on that fateful evening when he had taken Charlot's place at their rendezvous, the night from which all that had happened to her since had stemmed.

On their way back to the hotel he took her arm—a small intimacy which, for once, was not laid on for the benefit of an audience. As he walked beside her, matching their paces, his thigh often brushed hers, a closeness of involuntary touch which excited her. She was trembling slightly when, in the foyer, he assumed that she would go to their room before him, by taking the key from Reception and handing it to her without a word as to when he would join her, or indeed whether he intended to give her time to escape from him in sleep, genuine or faked. As she went up in the elevator she had still to wonder whether he had ordered a suite with two bedrooms in order to feel free to isolate himself in his or to invade hers. Then she remembered his scarcely veiled hint that he would claim his rights of her, and felt as fearfully certain as she was tremulously elated that she was to be allowed no interval of grace, that he would approach her that night. And when he did, he would know—— Know her, not for the woman he thought her, but for the one she really was. And that she wanted—desperately.

He could not have allowed her to precede him for long and must have come in while she was in her bathroom with the water running, for when she came through in nightgown and slippers he was already in his robe, superintending the drawing of a champagne cork by a room-service waiter.

The man bowed himself out. Dracon passed her a wineglass and lifted his own to her before inviting her to sit beside him on the brocade-covered couch of their sitting-room. Tara sipped the wine gratefully. Whatever was to come, the headiness induced by champagne should help. Dracon's toast of 'To what we may have achieved by our marriage' told her nothing of his immediate intentions, and of what he might be thinking there was nothing to be read in the long intense gaze he had turned on her.

Embarrassed by it, she shook her hair forward to make a curtain to hide behind. But Dracon reached to loop it back. 'It's a little late for modesty, isn't it?' he enquired. 'For good or ill, we are committed, you and I.' And then, 'What are you afraid of? After all, I am only a man—like all the others. And as the American, Benjamin Franklin, is alleged to have said, "In the dark, all cats are grey."'

Tara saw how his thought was trending now. Swallowing on a painful lump in her throat, she corrected him, 'It doesn't apply. He said it of all the women with whom he had been intimate.'

Dracon nodded agreement. 'I know that. But couldn't it equally refer to the several men a woman has known? Ten—twelve—a score—give or take a man or two, what matter? Except that'—his nonchalant tone suddenly turned savage—'except that you, Tara Leloupblanc, have finished counting us in numbers or in francs or in dollars or sterling. From now on *I* am your last grey cat whom you *will* distinguish from the rest!'

Now she was frightened. For something—anything to do, she took another sip from her glass, only for him to take it from her and to set aside his own. She looked at him pleadingly. 'You don't——' she began. 'There's something you don't——' And then, as he took her roughly by the shoulders and drew her to her feet, '*Please!*' she begged.

She had tried to envisage this scene too often to have hoped for any of the honeymoon gentleness he had never yet shown her except in public. In anger or contempt of her he had always turned as feral as his name. But in this moment of reality she had had to try to reach him with words, though sensing already that he was beyond allowing her to utter them; beyond wasting any of his own.

In a silence that she felt was a menace in itself he gathered her up, cradled her, one arm round her shoulders, and carried her to her room and to her bed. He lifted her shoulders again, far enough to draw down her nightgown from them, and at the instinctive woman's movement of her hands to cover her breasts, said, 'You would find darkness kinder, perhaps,' and switched off the bedside lamp.

The window curtains were thick; as he had brought her in he had kicked-to the door to the lighted lounge, and in the eclipse he had granted her, he lay beside her and took her into his arms.

She shrank again there, dreading the moment of truth soon to be upon them of which he had not let her warn him. A long shudder coursed through her and momentarily he drew back from her. But then, with what she supposed was expertise born of long practice, he was touching her hair, tilting her chin, dropping feather kisses from her ear-lobe to the corner of her mouth in a love-play which was as enticingly arousing as it was foreign to any approach for which she had been prepared.

Her spirit glowed to it, reluctantly grateful to whatever experience had taught him that savage assault was not the only way to tame a woman to his will. But though his gentleness was wooing her heart and her mind to responsive surrender, her body still shrank in fear of the unknown. At one of the supreme moments for which she had been made, her limbs were cold, her body felt as if it was about to knot in cramp, and she could not control the ague of shivering which shook the length of her spine.

Dracon could not but be aware of her recoil. He sat up, resting on one hand, looking down at her. 'What is it?' he asked. 'Why are you afraid? And of what?'

She could have been frank with his unwonted kindness. She could have said, 'Of this. Of you. I'm a coward, and for me it's the first time.' Or she could have denied she was afraid, have set her teeth and let him find out, as he inevitably must, that her untouched virginity had waited for him alone.

But she found herself with courage for neither. Disarmed and vulnerable, near to tears, she waited for him to press his question again and to insist on an answer. But he did not. Accustomed to the darkness now, she could see that he was watching her thoughtfully, his look unreadable, except that it was speculative rather than hostile. Tentatively she put out a hand in the direction of his shape, looming above her, but dropped it emptily when he ignored it.

'I'm s-sorry,' she chattered through her teeth, and again, 'Please——' without knowing what she was asking of him—to which his response was to pull up the coverlets to her chin. Stating, not asking, 'You are tired,' he said.

Drowning, she clutched at the straw. 'Yes, a—a little.'

'—And crying.' In covering her, his hands had touched her cheek, damp, not with the tears she had managed to hold back, but with a cold sweat which was beading the whole of her body now. She shook her head in fierce denial and hid her face in the pillow, torn between praying for him to go and longing for him to stay—and be kind.

He had gone round to her side of the bed, and she

was aware that for several moments he stood there in silence. Then with a sound like a rueful laugh—a *laugh*?—he said, '*You* should cry? Me, I am holding a bundle of damp squibs on the Fourteenth of July!' And then, 'However, what did I expect? We will talk in the morning.'

Then he was gone. His own door closed on the strangled cry of 'Dracon!' which she sent after him.

There was to be no talk in the morning. All night Tara had been fighting the rage of fire and ice in her veins. Soon after midnight she had got up to fling back the curtains on to the cool night air; her journey back to bed was a tottering progress, and when she lay down again her limbs were craving warmth to still their quaking.

Thought which began coherently turned to hazy muddle. People from her present and past merged incomprehensively; were, in turn, a waiter, her father, an olive-skinned Frenchwoman, a girl friend not seen since their schooldays; more clearly, Mathilde, and Dracon who plagued her with questions she could not answer, and who had vanished after making a cryptic remark with no point to it at all ...

The Fourteenth of July. The French National Day. Dancing in the streets. Parades. Spectacles. Fireworks at night—rockets, Catherine wheels, humble squibs. *Damp* squibs? Her mind wrestled with a problem, the solution of which made no sense when she found it, in that a load of sparklers too damp to light spelled disappointment to the hand which held them. But disappointment—and Dracon Leloupblanc? For him, calculated action, manoeuvre, yes; but accepted disappointment and Dracon did not jell.

She started in and out of feverish sleep and when at last she woke to daylight she couldn't lift her head from the pillow. She stirred restlessly, making the effort, and on lifting her heavy lids saw she was not alone. Dracon and another man stood at her bedside. When she looked up the stranger said 'Ah!' and reached to take her pulse.

'How long has she been like this?' he asked Dracon.

'I called you at once when I realised she was in high fever.'

'No symptoms last night? Nor during the night?'

'None that I noticed. This morning she was talking in her sleep.'

'Saying what?'

'Nonsense I couldn't understand.'

'H'm—mind wandering. Well, she must have picked up a fast-working virus, but she should respond to antibiotics quite soon. You would like me to send a nurse to her, *monsieur*?'

'Please, doctor.' Dracon smoothed back Tara's damply clinging hair before they turned away. As they reached the door she caught the words '*lune de miel*' and she registered vaguely, before she drifted off again, that Dracon must have been telling the doctor they were on their honeymoon.

Over the next three days she was dosed, fed with

liquids and left to sleep with increasing peace. Soeur Yvonne, one of the hotel nurses, was kind and skilful; another nurse sat with her during her first two nights of fever. Dracon, who had moved out of the suite for the nurses' benefit, came often to see her, telling her he was using his days to good business purpose instead of entertaining her round Paris, and on the fourth day she was sitting in a chair, her temperature normal, when he came.

Soeur Yvonne was there to witness his taking both her hands and his light kiss on her lips, and when he and the nurse exchanged their daily joke about Tara's 'spoiling' of the honeymoon by her illness, she smiled obediently at it.

They travelled to Bordeaux the next day, by air instead of by train. Before their flight Dracon installed her in the departure lounge while he went to the bar for the champagne suggested by the doctor as a tonic for her convalescent appetite. But in the constant to-and-fro and noise Tara could not concentrate on her magazine and was watching and listening instead.

Suddenly she bent her head again to the article she had been reading. But too late. The familiar figure of Ninon Chauvet was on its way towards her from across the lounge. Tara thought quickly. Dracon had forecast that the local gossip columns would have ensured that Isray—which also meant Ninon—would have heard of their marriage. But perhaps, if Ninon had been in Paris——?

Ninon, however, said she had only flown in that day

to see her dressmaker and would be returning on Dracon's and Tara's flight. She was clad in elegant travel gear of black silk tailored pants and shirt and a harlequin-squared black and white cloak. Without preliminary, except the conventionally proffered hand, she accosted Tara's convalescent wanness with, 'Really, for a new bride you look overtired—Madame Leloupblanc! Exhausted by Dracon's ardours? Or disappointed that he showed none?' and then waited for Dracon, followed by a barman, to add to him, 'Dracon, *mon brave*, if you had to marry your glamorous stranger clandestinely, you are too much of a public figure to do it in your own home city. All the local matrons with hopeful single daughters are furious with you— quite furious! And Mathilde, you will find, is *hurt*.'

Dracon said levelly, 'There was nothing particularly secret about it. But with no close family to invite to it, Tara wanted a quiet ceremony, and I fell in with that.'

Ninon's eyes widened. 'You allowed her to make the decision? Extraordinary!' she marvelled. 'But I have been telling her, she isn't looking at all well. To what erotic tortures have you put her, one wonders? Or'—archly—'shouldn't one ask?'

Dracon said shortly, 'She contracted some kind of fever on our first day here.' He poured from the tray the man had set down. 'You will drink with us? You are on this flight? Where are you sitting?'

They compared boarding passes to the first class cabin, finding, to Tara's relief, that Ninon would not be within conversation distance. But at Bordeaux

Ninon asked for a lift in Dracon's car which he had had sent for him.

'I must drop Tara at home first,' he told her.

Ninon smiled. 'But naturally! And Tara, leaving to shop in Paris and returning to the château as its mistress—this I must see! Mathilde, I predict, will soon forgive you for your little *coup*, and Elaine, starry-eyed with love herself, will not blame you at all. But Charlot —well, Charlot could react as he did to your engagement. Curious'—she mused—'he behaved so badly that evening that a mere onlooker could have supposed he was jealous.'

'Jealous of whom?' Dracon's question was sharp.

'Of you. Of Tara.'

'With what cause—when he and Elaine are so close?'

'Ah, but are they—recently? I thought I had noticed——'

'And are making mischief of a situation which doesn't exist?' Dracon had started the car, but stopped it in order to look round at her in the back seat. 'I warn you, Ninon, if you attempt to drive even an imaginary wedge between Charlot and Elaine, I shall hold you responsible for any consequences to her health. You hear?' Turning front again, he moved off.

Ninon gasped. 'Are you *threatening* me, Dracon?' she demanded on a high, provocative note.

'You should know,' he said over his shoulder with a finality which Tara recognised only too well, but which she welcomed for the silencing of Ninon for the moment.

What had been—or was still—the relationship between them? Tara wondered. Did Dracon seek solace and escape from his business affairs with Ninon, as she claimed? If so, his public manner with her being so caustic and arrogant, it could only be a love-hate bond, surely, though those, Tara knew, could make for unbreakable ties over the years. *Were* there such ties between Dracon and Ninon? Or—hopefully—had he genuinely taken Ninon's measure, knew her for what she was, and could deal with any danger from her?

If so—and the bitter irony of the thought struck Tara almost with amusement—she had sold her own birthright of freedom to save Dracon from a would-be tigress without any claws. And he had saddled himself with a wife he didn't love for an equally quixotic purpose. They were partners in folly, he and she. If only they were nearer to each other in sympathy, they could compare notes on it, and share their commiseration, however little else they had in common!

At the château they were greeted warmly by Mathilde who, if she had been disappointed of an elaborate wedding, gave no sign of it. She made a show of scolding Dracon, but her welcome to Tara as 'one of us' was all Tara could have hoped for if she had really become a Leloupblanc by right of a genuine courtship and consummated love match with the head of a clan as diehard and feudal as it was rooted and proud.

Elaine seemed as pleased as Mathilde. Charlot was not at home, and Mathilde, evasive as to his possible whereabouts, seemed glad to switch to practicalities when Ninon, showing no hurry to leave with Dracon, mischievously suggested that the château's sleeping arrangements would need adjusting in the light of Dracon's elopement. Had Mathilde considered that?

'Of course,' Mathilde assured her, and turned to Dracon. 'You will be moving with Tara into the blue suite when it is ready?'

'Which it isn't yet.'

'It could have been, if you had warned me earlier. But when you told me to order the decorators, I thought you meant there to be plenty of time before your wedding. As it is, they have only just begun work on it, and it could take some time. You should apologise to Tara for there being no *chambre de noces* ready for her. A fine homecoming indeed for you, my dear,' Mathilde added to Tara. 'I am so sorry!'

Dracon said, 'When we commissioned the decorators, I didn't know Tara would want so private a wedding——'

'Nor be in such a hurry?' But as no one glanced Ninon's way, only Tara, sitting nearest to her, could have heard her whispered, insolent question as Dracon went on,

'But it doesn't matter, as it happens. Tara won't mind staying in her own room for a while, and I'll move into the one next door to her.'

'That's what I thought,' Mathilde agreed happily,

but this time they all heard Ninon when she quoted, as if reciting a piece she had learned, '*Partout où le loup dirige, la meute y poursuivra*,' translating for Tara, ' "Where the wolf leads, the pack will follow." The family motto, *chérie*, and Dracon, your chosen wolf, who dictates, without a nod to you, where you will sleep, and how, on your first night in your own home!' She shook her head in mock-sympathy. 'Straws in the wind, I'm afraid; it won't be long now before he has you trained into the pack and following blindly. However, good luck, as my wedding wish to you. You may need all you can get.'

She stood then, gathered her things and told Dracon, 'Please take me home.'

'Willingly.' He followed her to the door, but on the threshold she turned.

'I shan't keep him long,' she promised. 'How would I *dare*?'

Mathilde shook her head, frowning. 'Ninon presumes too far with Dracon. One could almost suppose she resented his marrying you without asking her permission!'

'Is there any reason why she should mind?' Tara asked carefully.

'Only perhaps, being one who needs to be the only woman on any man's horizon, she fears that she may lose place with him.' Mathilde added, as if in apology for this criticism of Ninon, 'You see, I know her rather well. We have been neighbours for a long while, and though Henri, my husband, liked her and found her amusing, I have never felt very sure of her warmth of heart for any of us.'

And with cause, thought Tara in pity, remembering Ninon's brazen admission of Henri Leloupblanc's infidelity, a sword of Damocles she still held over the family's good name. She would use it, she had threatened, and she was capable of it out of sheer malice, Tara was convinced.

Mathilde was saying, 'Before you went away, I spoke to Dracon about our leaving—Charlot and Elaine and I—when you were married. But he refused to hear of it. Charlot and Elaine, when they make a home of their own, yes. But while Ninon owns and remains in the dower house, I must stay, he said. You do not mind, my dear?'

'*Mind?*' Impulsively Tara rose and went to hug her, touched by her faith in Charlot's and Elaine's future together, and glad to have her as an ally in her own uncharted future with Dracon. 'Yes, please stay,' she begged her, 'for just as long as it suits you. I—need you,' she added in appeal.

Mathilde nodded. 'You love Dracon and he loves you, but you are just a little afraid—hm?' she asked.

Tara looked away. 'A little,' she admitted. 'It has all been so—whirlwind.'

Mathilde laughed then. 'But the swift and sure courtships, they are the best!' she declared. 'And one could see at a glance that you were a prize Dracon meant to win against all comers. Sometimes I wish he were not so strong-minded, asking no one's advice and going his own way, but when he set his heart on you, he certainly knew what he was about—— Why, my dear, what is it?' she broke off as Tara, ashamed as never before in her life, burst into tears, brushing them from her cheeks in a weak effort at control.

'Just that you—all of you—are so much kinder than I deserve,' she stammered. 'You don't know——'

'—Enough about you in so short a time?' Mathilde finished for her. 'Nonsense! Whoever does know all about someone before loving them? A lot of the "knowing for certain" has to come later; in the meantime instinct and trust are good enough. Come now, tell me—you do not know Dracon very well yet? In many ways he is an enigma to you? But can you deny that you love him for what he has shown of himself so far? Come along, if you think you can, look me in the face and try!'

Tara looked up through a mist of tears. 'I can't,' she admitted.

'As I knew.' Mathilde nodded, satisfied. 'In the same way, we can love you on trust, and hope you can love us. But now you are still weak and tired, or you would not want to weep for happiness, and so I am going to send you to bed with a hot *tisane* inside you, to sleep for tonight alone.'

'Oh—Dracon may expect——' Tara felt she must protest.

'If he does, I shall bar your door,' declared Mathilde stoutly.

Tara laughed shakily. 'Not literally, I hope?'

'No. With my tongue. I think it should serve,' said Mathilde.

Whether or not Dracon came to her room that night Tara was not to know, for after the *tisane*, reputedly a lemon-flavoured herb tea, but into which Mathilde must have slipped something more potent, she slept dreamlessly until morning, waking to a lovely day to which her spirit lifted.

She looked at her two rings, the antique ruby circlet which guarded the slim gold wedding ring; told herself in wondering awe, 'I am married to Dracon,' and suffered a little less guilt than she had overnight. Dracon had had his way; had engaged himself to her and had married her, leaving him no further threat to hold over her in order to achieve the ends she was convinced must fail with Charlot.

For his own self-fulfilment in a son by her he meant to make her his wife in more than name—he had said so—and loving him as she did, she wanted him, needed him, even on his own coldblooded terms. And perhaps ... perhaps, when she had found the courage to lead him to learn the truth about herself, though it wouldn't make him love her, they might achieve some friendship and tolerance, for which she would gladly settle as the price she must pay for the shelter of his beloved shadow.

He came to take her to breakfast, saying he had stayed to talk business with Ninon and that Mathilde had persuaded him not to disturb her.

Business? thought Tara jealously. 'Did she want to discuss another offer for her land?' she asked.

'Not this time,' said Dracon. 'She has another problem with it now, with which I won't bother you. Charlot was home when I came back,' he went on. 'I have seen to it that he understands the future position very clearly. But I expect you to underline it—in my presence. As I've reminded you before, I have no evidence that you have ever discouraged him——'

'You have my word!'

'I should still like it spelled out to him in front of me—that our marriage puts an end to his calf hopes of you, because whatever interest you may have had in him is dead. I have told him myself that he had better look now to Elaine and to his work, but the final rejection which will convince him must come from you, must be *seen* to come from you.'

'But that's too cruel!' Tara protested. 'I couldn't do it, with you looking on. And even you can't order his feelings like that.'

'I can order his behaviour under my roof and towards my wife; I can also expect proof that you are sincerely on my side in this.'

'But if the only proof you will accept is to hear me turning him down in so many set words that you would approve, no doubt, then I'm afraid you will not get it. He knows already that there was only friendship between us——'

'So you've said, but I don't forget that you came here with the express purpose of seducing him into something more,' Dracon put in cuttingly.

'Only—then—to make you believe we were closer than we were. But not—we've been over all this before!—not after I knew about Elaine. And since then I've done all that our so-called engagement asked of me, and I'm prepared to—to honour our marriage. So isn't it enough that I've mortgaged my future to you, without being forced to humiliate Charlot in front of you, to give you your "proof"? You must see it's asking too much of either him or me?' she appealed.

Dracon scorned, ' "Too much", to want to be sure that I have at least your intentions of loyalty?'

'You *can* be sure! And I will see Charlot—but alone.'

'If I am not to be present, you needn't trouble yourself. You have seen him alone before, and with what result for Elaine? Why should I hope that another cosy tête-à-tête with him would do any more for her?' he countered.

They had reached the table on the courtyard where they breakfasted on fine mornings. As he pulled out her chair for her, Tara muttered, 'You've never trusted me in anything I've ever said or done. Will you ever?'

'Just as much, probably, no more and no less, than you trust me, my dear.'

Sitting now, she looked round and up at him. 'Why, when haven't I?' she asked.

He shrugged. 'On occasion. For example, think back to our wedding night and remember,' he advised obliquely.

'Our——? What do you mean?'

But Mathilde and Elaine were coming out from the house, and he went round the table to do the same courtesy for them.

CHAPTER EIGHT

LOOKING back, Tara realised she had only a vague, fever-racked memory of her wedding night. She could remember her fear of an intimacy which for some reason Dracon had spared her, but little more after he had left her, and nothing which could have led him to believe she did not trust him. Earlier she had been there, dangerously excited, waiting for him, and he had been kind. She could not remember having said anything to repulse him, and such mistrust as she had felt had been of her own cowardice in face of his learning that about her which he did not know.

When he came to her tonight—as surely he would soon, now she was well again?—she would argue that she had trusted him enough to marry him, hadn't she? And from there, if he agreed, there should be some way, however difficult, to find courage enough for the rest.

But he did not come that night, nor for so many thereafter that her bewildered need of him at last ran out of excuses for him. He had warned her that, however calculated on his side, their marriage was to be in more than name; he had shown her more than once the latent, unbridled passion of which he was capable; though against her will at first, he had inexorably drawn her to him in yearning, primitive response. But now he had punishingly abandoned her for no reason of which she could feel guilty, and for the first time now she began to have doubts of his motives.

Supposing his policing of Charlot and his care for Elaine's happiness were very secondary to his determination to avenge himself on the kind of woman he believed her to be? Supposing that from the beginning he had lured her by stages into a marriage which he had presented to her as her duty, but which he had meant all along should be her trap?

If that were so, then she had good cause to doubt him, and it made an empty nonsense of her own need to save him from Ninon's scheming. For if he were as devious as that, he deserved no help from her. But though she prayed that he wasn't, the embittered thought nagged, steeling a pride which would *not* plead, nor explain, nor betray to him her unfulfilled craving to earn the title of 'wife' at his hands. No one, least of all he, should know what her nightly banishment meant to her in torment of mind and the ceaseless Why? of her despair.

Outwardly and publicly she could not fault his manner. It was attentive and thoughtful, from the single flower which appeared without fail on her early-morning tray to the apparently genuine interest he showed in her doings when he was not with her. Just as he had predicted he could, he played the newly married husband well, and resolved as she was to claim no grievance against him, she took her cue from his various moods, biding her time until he must, she argued, reveal his intentions towards her.

She felt sure that Mathilde suspected nothing of the chasm between them; her practical concern with the readying of the *chambre de noces* for their use was one proof of that. Another was her urging of Dracon that very soon he must throw a big party as a make-peace gesture to their friends for the haste and secrecy of his marriage—a suggestion which he had skilfully by-passed to date.

Charlot matched a front of distant non-interest with a continuing hurtful neglect of Elaine. He attempted no contact with Tara with which Dracon could quarrel, and as Dracon had scorned and distrusted any over-tures of hers to Charlot, she saw no reason for re-monstrating with him again.

Elaine, increasingly listless and withdrawn, kept her own counsel until one day, by the swimming-pool, she said quietly to Tara,

'I have told Charlot that he and I are—finished. He does not want me, and I—I cannot bear any more——' She stared out over the sunlit pool, adding, 'Sometimes I wish I could not swim.'

Shocked and anxious, Tara protested, 'Elaine, you mustn't say or let yourself think like that!'

'Why not? It would be easy—just to walk into deep water and——'

'*No!*' Such abandonment to misery was beyond Tara's experience and she did not know how to deal with it. Deciding it was too late now to deny Charlot's only too obvious change of heart, she urged, 'Listen, you are desperately unhappy over Charlot, and no wonder. Dracon is angry with him, and Tante Mathilde and I have tried to persuade you that he is only passing through a bad mood. But now he behaves shabbily to you all the time, it has been left to you to do the brave thing—to tell him you have had enough. And if you have found the courage for that, you certainly have all it takes to cut the loss of him—and go on. Do you see?'

'Go on to—what?'

'The rest of your life. Getting cured. You are improving all the time.'

'Because I've wanted to get well and whole—for Charlot. I've stood all the drills, and Dracon's rules about exercises and rest, and keeping boring nursery hours, for Charlot's sake. But I'm not a child any more. I'm grown-up and I love Charlot, and I *was* willing to work at—everything. But if he doesn't want me any more, who else will?'

Tara said, 'I won't tell you, "Nonsense. Of course someone will," because I don't think that worries you much now. It is Charlot you love now, and Charlot who has hurt you now. And it is the immediate now—tomorrow, the day after, next week—that you wonder how to live through, isn't it?'

Elaine nodded. 'Having to see him. Having to stay here. Watching him go out. Hearing his car. That is why——' She threw another brooding glance at the pool.

Tara thought quickly. 'That is going to be the worst of it for you? Having to be here yourself, and seeing him around, coming and going every day? Are you thinking it might be easier if he weren't here for a time? Or if you weren't? she asked.

'I have to be,' Elaine said dully. 'Dracon wouldn't trust me to keep to my routine for a day anywhere else. And this is Charlot's home. He couldn't afford to live away from here until Dracon promotes him in the firm, which he would have done, Charlot thought, if we married. But yes, it would help, perhaps, not to have to see him or listen for him all the time.' She stood, picked up her towel and sunglasses, then added with heart-stirring candour, 'Though if he went away, I should always be wondering where he was, what he was doing, and which girl—or girls—he was taking out!'

'I know.' Tara nodded her understanding. 'And I know how it hurts.'

On her way up the path to the house, Elaine turned on her heel and looked back. 'How can you?' she accused. 'There is nothing wrong with you. Dracon loves you and you are married to him. You haven't an idea what it is like for me.' She turned again and limped on.

So much for Dracon's conviction that Charlot could be forced back to Elaine! thought Tara. And so much for her own committal to Dracon which had drawn her along with him. Now he had to know how abysmally they had failed, driving Elaine to wild thoughts of suicide, and Charlot—who could tell where?

Whether or not he planned it so, lately she was finding time alone with Dracon difficult to achieve. Since their marriage Ninon did not visit the château so often, but Dracon went frequently to the dower house, sometimes spending most of an evening there, explaining his errand only by saying that Ninon had business problems which he was helping her to iron out.

'Real problems?' Tara wanted jealously to ask, and would have done if she hadn't felt that to sink to low sneers put her on to Ninon's own level. She deplored having to line up behind Ninon, but that night after dinner, knowing he had gone to the stables and would be coming back, she waited in her room by the open french window. She heard him coming and beckoned to him. He came in. 'Permission to smoke?' he asked, indicating the cheroot between his fingers, and leaned easily against the window frame when it was lit. Before Tara could speak he said,

'I must make time to give Le Loup Garou more exercise. He is getting very mettlesome and restive, and that's bad for him—as for any frustrated male.'

'Doesn't Ninon Chauvet take him out for you? I've seen her riding him,' said Tara.

'Yes. But she is rather preoccupied just now.'

'And you won't let Charlot ride him, Elaine says?'

'*Mon dieu*, no! Especially in their present bestially stubborn moods, they could well do each other an injury.'

'Yes, well,' Tara hurried in quickly, 'we have got to talk about Charlot—and about Elaine. So far she has done her best to hide it, but she has got to such a point of despair that though she has been brave enough to free Charlot, she has gone all to pieces, and today she hinted to me of not wanting to go on; of having thought of suicide.'

Tara had meant to shock Dracon and hoped his silence showed she had done so. At last, looking at the ash on his smoke, he said, 'She can't be serious. At her age a threat of suicide is often only a dramatic attitude. When Charlot comes to his senses, she will forget she ever felt that way.'

Tara flared, 'Believe that if it helps you! But she is *not* striking an attitude. I don't say she would attempt it, but she's in the kind of depths where she could. It's a cry for help, and even you must admit she and Charlot are as far apart as ever. Your object lesson to him hasn't worked.'

'It is early days yet.'

For the first time in her experience of him, Dracon seemed on the defensive, and she pressed home her advantage. 'It's *late* days for Elaine,' she declared. 'Late enough for her to have broken with Charlot and to be on the verge of breaking her own heart. Just how blind can you be, that you can still hope your wishful thinking for her can have any of the result you planned?'

Dracon said tersely, 'Not as blind as you imply. But unlike you, I'm prepared to give Charlot time to learn the object lesson of your marriage to me. However, as you seem to have assumed charge of the situation, what do you suggest I do about it?'

Asking her advice—this wasn't like him! Tasting power, Tara began, 'You could——' and then broke off. 'No,' she contradicted herself, 'you could accept for once that there's nothing you can do, except to stop *doing*. You've already done it all—and failed. Involved me, manoeuvred Charlot and Elaine as if they were pieces in a board game, and it's high time you realised that even you can't try to play God to other people's lives and get away with it indefinitely!'

'I see. And if this negative counsel is all you can offer me, do you mind if I conclude you only wanted to sneer "I told you so"? Or, more bitingly, "You have failed for once, Dracon Leloupblanc—how does it feel?" Could that be so?' he insinuated.

That in part it was, was more than Tara could bring herself to admit, and at a loss for a reply to the taunt, she said nothing.

Dracon waited, his brows lifted in enquiry. Then, 'As I thought,' he said, levered himself upright and left her. In a battle of wills and bitter words he had won again.

After that she did not expect anything of her nights

spent alone, with him only on the far side of a wall, of a door that he could open, but never did. They were at deadlock, all of them. He and she went through the motions of newly-married comradeship. Elaine obediently swam and rode and walked and jerked to her physiotherapist's orders. Charlot came and went, spending the minimum possible time at home, confiding in no one and discouraging any approach. They were so many marionettes, Tara thought. Where was it all going to end?

Mathilde, though she worried openly about the impasse between Charlot and Elaine, remained her capable, domesticated self with nothing to hide from her world until, one quiet afternoon, Tara came upon her, unusually idle, in the belvedere. She was staring out unseeingly at the garden while her fingers pleated restlessly at the sheet of paper in her lap.

She turned with a start when Tara joined her. The paper fluttered to Tara's feet and she saw the formal block lettering it contained as she handed it back. Mathilde took it, smoothing it now, preparatory to folding it. Then she said impulsively, 'A letter. An unpleasant one.' She hesitated. 'But you are one of us now. Will you read it?'

'A private letter? Do you want me to?' Tara asked.

'Please. Dracon must see it too.'

Tara took it. Typically an anonymous screed, it read: 'How the friends of the great Leloupblanc family will enjoy the story of how Henri Leloupblanc took and flaunted a mistress under his wife's nose for years!

Under *your* nose, Mathilde Leloupblanc, and you
never guessed, did you? But now your proud pack
leader has taken a wife, how pleased will he be when
this ripe little scandal gets back to her by way of any
of those who will hear it very soon? Especially in view
of his own interest in his late uncle's left-over lady?
But though names will be named, please, dear
Mathilde Leloupblanc, do not think of this as blackmail. It is simply a paying-off of old scores.' There was
no signature.

Tara exclaimed with distaste, 'What a disgusting
document!' only to be surprised by Mathilde's rueful
half-smile as she replied,

'It is, and it would have given me quite a shock, if
it told me anything I didn't know already!'

'Then you knew about——?'

'About my husband and Ninon Chauvet? Oh yes. At
first I was hurt. Then I was angry, and then I was as
amused as they thought they could be, laughing behind
my back. Yes, it is Ninon to whom this person refers,
and though it can't affect *me* now, I am so sorry, my
dear, that it should put doubt of Dracon into your
mind. For believe me, there is nothing guilty going on
between him and Ninon. He is far too much in love
with you. And so'—Mathilde tapped the letter—'this
poor deluded writer is left holding *two* damp squibs
she (or he?) did not expect. She reveals nothing which
shocks me, and even less, I assure you, that can hurt
you. As for Ninon—well, am I a very wicked woman,
I wonder, if I cannot care too much, should the truth

about her and Henri get out?' Mathilde concluded
with something of a malicious glint in her candid eyes.

(Damp squibs? *Damp squibs?*) For Tara the words
just touched a chord of memory and were gone. Aloud
she said slowly, working out her intuitive thought, 'Do
you know, as soon as the writer learns that she has told
you nothing new about your husband and Ninon, I
don't think the story will go any further.'

Mathilde puzzled, 'But we don't know who is the
writer!'

'I think I do.'

'You?'

Tara drew a long breath. 'I believe it's Ninon herself. 'No'—she put up a hand to silence Mathilde's
astonished denial—'this is why. Listen——'

Mathilde listened. At the end of Tara's account of
Ninon's threat of exposure of the story, she questioned,
'She could be so jealous of Dracon's marrying you
that she could try to injure him with the scandal in the
family, as well as me?'

'I'm afraid so.' Discarding all discretion, Tara
added, 'From almost our first meeting, she has never
made any secret of hoping she could marry him herself.
In consequence, she and I have never—got on.'

'Though without our guessing it. Oh dear, poor
Ninon, one can almost be sorry for her when Dracon
has to deal with her over this!'

'You feel you must show him her letter?'

'Without doubt, if she is not to spread the story
around. He must face her with it.'

'She could deny having written it.'

'In face of the threat she made to you? And Dracon will believe *you*,' Mathilde averred with a conviction Tara wished she herself could feel. Out of her own experience she said, 'If she does love him and has thought that he loves her, he could be harsher with her than she deserves. Women in love aren't always—responsible.'

Mathilde smiled. 'You are too generous, *chérie*, being loved and in love yourself. Me, though I have long forgiven Ninon for the past, in this piece of nastiness, though I can almost feel sorry for her, I cannot *quite* bring myself to spare her Dracon's anger!'

But Dracon was to have news for them which almost eclipsed theirs for him.

The three of them were taking coffee after dinner when he told Mathilde, 'If you wish, it needn't be long before you can pack your bags and move into the dower house. Ninon is leaving it at the end of the month.'

Mathilde and Tara exchanged blank glances. Mathilde questioned, 'Leaving? Why?'

'She has agreed to sell it to me.'

'But—the estate? What about that?'

'Ah, the estate!' Dracon turned to Tara. 'You will remember that when I told you I should like to own it and work it for vines, I said then I thought I could bide my time for persuading Ninon to sell?'

Tara said, 'Your actual words were that, though

there were spurs to which any woman would answer, you hadn't then found the right one for Ninon Chauvet.'

He made a show of admiration. 'What a computer memory! But yes, I did think that when she had failed to sell it elsewhere, she would name her price to me. She never has, so evidently—in her case—I have failed to use the right spur. But something I have known and she hasn't, is that time has been running out for her over the years, and it has caught up with her now.'

'Time?'

'Yes. By a very seldom invoked by-law of the region, land over a certain area left derelict and unproductive for a certain number of years must revert, at only its derelict value, to the local Land Commission, and the Isray land, as a saleable property, is now only within a few weeks of that deadline date.'

'Oh, Dracon, if she didn't know this, shouldn't you have warned her?' Mathilde protested.

His expression hardened. 'Why should I? As owner, she should have made it her business to learn the limitations of her ownership. Instead, she has sat there in her bijou oriental palace, watching the land destroy itself, refusing to allow me to relieve her of it, and lying to me from time to time, about fictitious offers she has had for it. No, I am willing to buy it from her now at its estimated value to me, which is higher than any figure she has yet claimed to have had, and that is all I owe her, however you, Tante Mathilde, may consider otherwise.'

Mathilde glanced again at Tara. 'But I don't——
That is, *we* don't, do we, Tara dear? You see, I have
had this—Tara, where is my bag? Ah, there it is——'
Opening it, she took the letter from it. 'I told Tara you
must see this, and I meant to show it to you tonight.
Read it, please, will you? It came by post,' she added
simply, as if in excuse for its having come at all.

They both watched as Dracon read. When she saw
he had finished Mathilde said, 'I am sorry you had to
learn this about Henri, Dracon. By his mistress it
means Ninon, I'm afraid, and though it speaks of
scandal you wouldn't want your friends or Tara to
know, it is also meant as a shock for me. Which it isn't,
because—well, I've known for years about—about
their affair.'

Dracon crumpled the paper, his fingers closing on it
like a vice. 'And so have I,' he said quietly. Too quietly,
Tara thought.

'*You* have?' Mathilde began to laugh shakily. 'To
think of Ninon's going to all this trouble to shock us
all, and drawing such a blank!'

'Ninon?' Dracon questioned.

'Yes.' As Dracon glanced at his closed fist, 'Yes, I
know it purports to be written by an enemy of Ninon's
as well as ours, but Tara is very sure Ninon sent it, because she has already warned Tara that she would
show up the scandal if——'

'If?' Dracon's echo was a question directed at Tara,
not his aunt.

Tara hesitated. 'I think—if and when you married
me,' she said.

'*If* I married you? Was there any doubt in her mind that I meant to?'

'She made it very clear to me she hoped it wouldn't happen; said she would go to any lengths to prevent it.'

'Her weapon being this scandal in the family?'

'Yes.' Tara did not think it necessary to elaborate on Ninon's abortive plan to smear her own reputation for the interest of the Leloupblanc circle of friends. Madame Fahier, bless her for a broadminded woman of the world, had brought her own brand of cynicism to scuttle that!

Dracon's inquisition continued. 'And giving you some reason, no doubt, for why she wanted to prevent it?'

'Because she was jealous of Tara.' It was Mathilde who answered that one. 'That is why she made her threat.'

'Though failing to intimidate you enough to make you cry off our engagement?' Dracon had again turned to Tara.

Her head went up proudly: 'As far as I know, I've never reacted very meekly to threats—from whatever quarter they've come,' she said, sending him a message she meant him to understand.

For a long moment his eyes claimed hers unreadably. Then, 'No,' he said. And then, 'I—see,' making the pause significant. And then, unfolding and smoothing the paper in his hand as Mathilde had done for its use in evidence, 'I rather think we needn't wait until the end of the month for vacant possession of the dower house. Ninon, if not her possessions, should be out of it within twenty-four hours at most.'

A witness against Ninon in a judicial enquiry— that's all I am to him, thought Tara in resentment of his soulless conduct of an affair which was charged with drama, if nothing else. She remembered his crushing of Ninon's letter in that steely grasp, and felt a stir of pity for her, as she and Mathilde heard him leave the house and start up his car.

Mathilde pondered, 'How strange, that Dracon should have known all this time! I suppose he thought I didn't know, and wouldn't upset me. *I* found out when I picked up a telephone extension and heard Henri speaking to Ninon, making a date, on the line. I was very bitter at the time, but I loved Henri, and I did nothing about it, for Charlot's and Elaine's sake.'

'And you have welcomed Ninon here since. How could you bear to?' Tara asked.

'Never really *welcomed* her,' Mathilde corrected. 'She assumed she had a right here; it is Dracon's house, not mine, and not knowing he would have understood why, I thought I couldn't refuse to know her any more. And that puzzles me a little,' she frowned, 'since he did know about her and Henri, why did he encourage her himself? There was a time when I thought he might be in love with her too, but never, of course, since he met you. So why?'

'I think,' said Tara slowly, 'he has always known what he wanted of her—the estate, and has probably had a lot of satisfaction from playing her—like a captive salmon—until he got it.'

Mathilde smiled. 'That is rather shrewd of you, dear—as if you are prepared to accept and love him for what he is. And he has some faults, you know, one of them being his wanting—and getting, and the worse the opposition, the surer the getting in the end. For that *is* Dracon Leloupblanc. He has to win.'

'Yes, I know,' said Tara.

Dracon gave no report on his interview with Ninon, and Charlot was the only one to see her before she left. At breakfast the next morning, a Saturday, when Dracon might go to the office but he did not, he announced that Ninon had rung him overnight to ask him to lunch with her.

'You are going?' Dracon asked.

'Why not? *You* may have trumped up some reason for getting her out of the dower house before she meant to go, but I've no quarrel with her, so why not?'

Dracon shrugged. 'As you please. No doubt she will appreciate a shoulder to weep on. And I only asked because I had meant you should lunch with me in the city, to meet a man who might be of use to you.'

'Huh, another of your sales-efficiency experts, brought in to teach me my job? No, thank you! On my free day, you can count me out,' said Charlot truculently.

'Very well. I'll phone and cancel.' Dracon turned to Tara. 'Shall we ride this afternoon? And dine somewhere in the city this evening?'

'I should like to.' It was the first outside date he had suggested since their latest clash over Elaine. Within minutes, an unwonted restraint with Charlot and an olive-branch for herself—this was Dracon in a new light which Tara wondered if she dare trust.

After luncheon she changed and went to wait for him at the stables, where only an under-lad was in charge.

'I shall be riding L'Etoile,' she told him. 'And Monsieur, of course, Le Loup——'

Agape, the boy looked up from his grooming of Elaine's grey, Dansette. 'But—but,' he stammered, 'Mademoiselle has *taken* Le Loup!'

'Taken——?' Tara dashed over to the half-door of the stallion's stall and looked over it. The stall was empty. White to the lips, she whirled round on the frightened lad. 'You *allowed* Mademoiselle to take him out? You know very well that Monsieur allows no one but himself to ride him!' she accused.

'Mademoiselle Chauvet rides him,' the boy defended.

'Yes, I'd forgotten,' Tara admitted. 'But not Monsieur Charlot, and certainly not Mademoiselle. How could you let her?'

'She made me understand she has permission.'

'How did she?'

'Well, she said Monsieur is worried that Le Loup has not enough exercise, which I know, and that she has offered to give him some. And so I think——'

'Wrongly,' snapped Tara. 'She would never have

got permission. But when was this? How long ago?'

'A—a quarter of an hour. A little more.'

'And which way did she take?'

'As usual when she rides Dansette—across the vine-yards, making for the woods, I suppose.'

The woods! The menace of low branches and slip-pery air-roots to Elaine on a strange mount—alone! Tara ordered, 'Saddle L'Etoile as quickly as you can. Monsieur was to meet me here, but you must tell him what has happened and ask him to follow.'

'What on?'

'Either of the others—Dansette, Filoselle.' Realising the boy was stupid through fright, she pitied him in face of Dracon's wrath, and threw him a crumb of consolation. 'Never mind. If Mademoiselle gave you to think it was all right, you weren't wholly to blame,' she told him as she mounted and rode out of the yard.

And that was a pretty grudging understatement, she thought as she put L'Etoile to a gallop. For how could a mere servant have been expected to resist Elaine, weighted down by the same despair as had prompted that death-wish glance at the swimming pool which Tara had read aright?

Elaine wasn't merely risking the awful hazards of riding the big horse. She had set out in a numb, un-reasoning search for them, Tara was convinced.

CHAPTER NINE

THERE was enough open view of the wide stretches of the vineyard to confirm that, with such a start, Elaine would have ridden further. Tara's mare had nothing of the speed of Le Loup, but surely, Tara prayed, Elaine would not dare to put him even to a canter. Unless—— But Tara did not want to pursue that thought, and tried instead to count upon sighting her on one of the forest rides which opened off the road beyond the estate boundary.

She tried several without success, wheeling and returning when the tracks disappeared in deeply shadowed undergrowth. She tried cross paths; rather hopelessly tried calling—until, on a much wider, more open sward she saw her quarry ahead on the horizon, the horse seemingly in control, and Elaine, with her awkward seat and twisted body, a grotesque silhouette against the sky.

Tara called again then, but Elaine either did not hear or did not heed, and Tara hurried L'Etoile forward, gaining a little while the stallion kept its pace. Purposely, as they neared, she did not call again, lest she startle Elaine, but suddenly, with a great harsh 'kraak, kraak' and a flash of white, a jay sped out from the bordering trees and across the track at just above Elaine's head height.

The stallion screeched a neigh, reared, came down, rocked on shuddering forelegs and hind, tossing Elaine from the saddle as if she were a rag doll, wheeled round and came plunging straight into the little mare's path.

Somehow Tara urged her into a dressage sidestep and another, and turned her about, so that she was tremblingly ready to run parallel as Le Loup came on. At a calculated moment Tara shortened her reins, half-stood in the stirrups—and reached.

At first Le Loup's bridle ran abortively through her gloved palm. Then it yielded with a sickening drag at her arm muscles, enabling her to jerk his head round and to keep her grip against his frenzied nursery-horse rocking on front legs and rear. At last he quietened, stood foaming and red-eyed while she spoke soothingly to him. But then it was L'Etoile's turn. Still frightened and excited by the stallion's scent, she plunged, un-seating Tara who went down between the two of them.

One foot was still caught in her stirrup. As she struggled to free it and managed to, one of eight random hooves caught her on the side of her head. The ground on which she lay was in quake—rolling in-sanely into mounds and valleys, and the sky was com-ing down, closing in on her. There were stars ... there was nothing ... And then, in a brief flash of con-sciousness which was not to last, Dracon was there, kneeling by her, pillowing her against his thigh and calling her by love-names he had never used to her before—'*Beloved*', 'Precious', 'My lovely one', and the sweet intimacy of '*mon chou*'—his 'cabbage'!

She was dreaming, of course. For there was no one about whom he needed to impress. Or was there? She was vaguely aware of two other grazing horses now. And was that Charlot? But no, it couldn't be. Charlot had gone to lunch with the enemy ... Now the ground was waving about again, and again there was nothing ...

When she came to she was on her own bed, though she wasn't undressed and it wasn't night. Her head was aching abominably and her eyes focused only slowly. They lighted upon Mathilde, who sprang from her chair and came over to her.

'I must have fainted,' Tara croaked.

'But only for a minute or two. You came round again, but Dracon brought the doctor to you there, in case either of you had broken anything and trying to move you did more harm than good.' Mathilde told her.

'Either of us?' The scene cleared for Tara. 'Oh— Elaine! I couldn't help her. Le Loup had already thrown her when——— Is she badly hurt?'

'Rather worse than you, dear. You must have learned how to fall, and you have only this lump the size of a *boule*—there, feel it—and the skin under your hair is hardly broken. But Elaine was kicked too, and has some broken ribs and a wrist. Anyway, Dracon had to decide to ride for the doctor himself, as Charlot was in such a state over her, and you were both put under sedation for long enough to get you home. The doctor took Elaine on with him to the hospital for X-rays to be done, and Charlot went with them. They may keep Elaine there. Dracon was with you until a few minutes ago, when he left me to watch you, while he went to arrange for the horses to be brought in. He will be back.'

'Then'—wonderingly—'he *was* there quite soon after I was thrown? And Charlot too? How?'

'Dracon was at the stables only a few minutes behind you. Charlot had had a furious row with Ninon, and he went down with Dracon. Poor young Martin, a jelly of fright, told Dracon what had happened and they followed to look for you—and found you, thank God,' said Mathilde fervently.

'But I had bungled things. Le Loup had taken fright and had already thrown Elaine when I managed to stop him and came off myself. Is Dracon very angry?' Tara appealed.

'Angry? With whom?'

'With Elaine for persuading Martin to saddle Le Loup for her. Which she did, you know; he wasn't to blame. And with me for—well, for my chasing after her madly without an idea of what to do, instead of waiting for him to put a proper rescue plan in hand.' (Or even for my knowing, when he refused to admit it, that Elaine had come so near to the edge of utter despair that she almost hoped for an accident on Le Loup.) But that thought Tara kept to herself. Mathilde couldn't be expected to understand how unreasoned and unjust Dracon's angers against her were apt to be.

As Mathilde showed when she echoed again, 'Angry? With you? Why should he be? My dear child, he was beside himself, when he thought you were badly hurt. I have never seen him so distressed, nor so grim.'

Grim, Tara thought she could believe. But distressed? Or yes, perhaps that too, over property he claimed publicly to value. Mathilde was continuing, 'In fact, I didn't know which of them, Charlot or Dracon, needed the more reassuring that neither of you was dead nor in danger of it. Charlot is being quite pitiful, calling himself unheard-of names for neglecting Elaine lately, when he loves her—*loves her*, he declares.' A little woman-wise smile played about Mathilde's lips as she added, 'You know, *chérie*, fear —for someone or something he loves beyond himself —can undermine a man's morale more surely than anything. He can go to pieces. So if *your* man ever shows himself afraid—it could happen, even to Dracon —remember that and be kind, won't you?'

'I can't imagine Dracon afraid of anything,' Tara murmured.

' "Afraid for", not "afraid of",' Mathilde corrected. She turned to speak to the opening door. 'Come in, Dracon. She is herself again—and needing to tell you so.'

Dracon came in. Tara looked at him anxiously, praying he would not overdo his concern for her in front of Mathilde. Momentarily she had been granted a glimpse of the fear of which Mathilde had spoken; the shock which had betrayed him into those endearments had been real enough for him to have meant them at the time. At that first sight of her on the ground between the threshing hooves, he *had* been afraid for her and had reacted with sweetnesses he might regret but which he had left for her treasuring. She didn't want them repeated for an audience.

She need not have worried. Dracon had not spoken before Mathilde left them. Tara put out a hand to him and he took it, held it.

'I'm all right now,' she said. 'Do I look a fright?'

'Rather one-sided as to the head. Are you in much pain?'

'Headachy, but it's going off.'

'And your other bruises?'

'I'm not conscious of them. Have I any?'

'Several minor ones, according to Doctor Matisse. You are going to be multi-coloured in a few days' time.'

Ordinary concern for her now. No unmanning fear. He was in perfect control, as always.

'How is Elaine?' she asked.

'We haven't heard yet. Charlot stayed at the hospital with her. He has been ringing from time to time, and he will again before he brings her home if he is allowed to.'

'Oh——' Tara looked down at their clasped hands. 'Has she been conscious? Able to talk? Has she said—why?'

'Yes. She came round on the way to the hospital,

found Charlot with her, holding her hand, and she confessed to him that she took Le Loup quite recklessly, not caring, even wanting him to throw her.' Dracon paused. 'Proving you were right and I was wrong. It *was* both a cry for help and a feeble tilt at suicide.' He stopped again. 'And we have failed, you and I. We haven't done anything for her that I hoped we might. It is fear for her—stark, cold fear of losing her that has brought and will bring Charlot to his senses. She has never hidden what she feels for him, and please God, this afternoon's work has shown him what she has always meant to him, long-term; that what they decided was the right thing for them when she was only a schoolgirl and before her illness is the right thing still and always will be.'

'But will this conviction last?' Tara doubted.

'One can only hope and believe. True, it might not, with you still in his background. But I've already taken steps about that.'

'Steps?' (To part from her? End their marriage before it had even begun?) Her heart seemed to plunge and turn over.

'Yes. This luncheon date I offered Charlot was with the owner of a fleet of pesticide-spraying aircraft in Algiers. He needs pilots and is prepared to take on Charlot. Not at an opening salary which will keep Elaine too, but I'll supplement that.'

As if she were coming up for air from deep water, Tara drew a long, grateful breath. 'You would release him from the firm?'

'As he has always claimed to want, and as Château

d'Isray expands into a viticulture of its own, I've decided it shan't carry malcontents. No, as soon as Elaine has recovered, they can both be in Algiers within a month.'

'But you let Charlot off the lunch. Does he know about this offer now?'

'Yes, I told him on my way down to the stables to meet you, I thought. He had turned up, mouthing fire, from his date with Ninon, who seems to have enjoyed a last fling at us by telling him in explicit detail all about her lengthy *amour* with his father. He stood that, he said, none too sure she wasn't lying. But when she went on to joke about how they had cuckolded Mathilde, then he saw red and—regrettably—slapped her face. Or perhaps not so regrettably,' Dracon corrected himself. 'I ought to have done it myself before now—and often.'

Tara questioned, 'You have seen through her all along?'

'I'd have thought that was obvious.'

'It hasn't been. You let her ride Le Loup, and you have invited her here, even though you knew about your uncle's affair with her.'

'Mostly she invited herself, and Le Loup needed the exercise. Any more evidence on the books?'

'Well—you have spent a lot of your time with her. And she told me you enjoyed going to the dower house to relax.'

'Relax? In that clutter of bamboo and bead curtains and brassware? But I needed to keep an eye on what she was up to, in case she did get a genuine offer for the estate and took it before the Land Commission threatened a forced sale, which wouldn't have suited me. Not that there was much danger, since no one would have given the absurd figures of the offers she claimed to have had made to her—knowing I wanted it and thinking she could hold me to indefinite ransom for it.' Dracon paused. 'Did she ever hint to you that she would have married me, had I asked her?'

'Yes. How do you know that was what she wanted?'

'Easy to guess she saw marriage as her weapon in reserve. What did you say when she told you she had it in mind? Pointed out that I was already engaged to you, I hope?'

'I—suppose so.'

'Even though I had forced the engagement on you, and you had no intention of its being a permanency if you could help it?'

'You had warned me that no one was to guess it wasn't a real engagement,' Tara reminded him.

'And so you held off Ninon in her role of temptress Eve, dangling the prize apple of the estate before me. In the circumstances, that was loyal of you,' he commented.

Tara disclaimed 'loyal' with a shake of her head and a grimace, because the movement had hurt. 'It was more that I didn't want you to marry Ninon on her terms,' she admitted.

'But with our emergency over, and our engagement

ended, why should you have cared whether I married
Ninon or not?'

Tara looked at him in reluctant awe of the skill with
which he had drawn her almost to the point of the
humiliating confession that she was jealous of Ninon,
jealous for love of him. 'I didn't like her,' she muttered lamely.

'Oh, come! Over the hills and free of a man who
had hijacked you, you would have grudged his marrying another woman for his own ends?'

'For *her* ends. I've told you, I didn't *like* her! Isn't
that enough reason? Do I have to——?'

'You have to—nothing.' Dracon withdrew his hand
and gave hers back to her, laying it palm down on her
breast. As if I were dead, she thought, petulant with
frustration. 'I'm all right. I want to come down to
dinner,' she said.

'No. You will stay here and dinner will be brought
to you.'

'But I want to see Elaine if they bring her back.'

'You shall. Charlot too, if you like. Mathilde will
come and help you to undress, and if you are good you
shall get up to see Elaine.' He turned to the door. 'I
won't trouble you again myself tonight,' he said.

At that, something broke for her, some floodtide of
need of him, of reckless, aching desire. He didn't want
her, but she had to crave something of him, something
more than those few love-words of his shock. She
pulled herself upright against her pillows. '*Please!*'
she begged of him. 'Please—come to see me again. If
—only to say goodnight!'

Dracon turned again and smiled. For once there were no reserves behind his eyes.

'I thought you would never ask!' he said.

After all, Charlot had to come home alone. Elaine, sedated for the pain of her cracked ribs and with her broken wrist in plaster had been kept for twenty-four hours' observation. But she had sent messages for them all through Charlot.

Mathilde brought him to Tara's room to deliver hers, then left them together, saying that on this, of all disrupted evenings, Dracon had chosen to ask some extra work of the maids, and she must go to superintend them.

'I told him that all this had held everything up; that the girls had their hands full and so had I, and surely this job—clearing up after the decorators—could wait. But he said he had expected to be rid of them before this. He was tired of the clutter they had left behind them, and if the clearing up meant extra work for Simone and Belle, he would make it worth their while to do it tonight. And so——' Mathilde shrugged expressively, 'well, you know what Dracon is!'

'Don't we all?' Charlot called after her as she bustled away. 'But I suppose I must learn not to crab him,' he added to Tara. 'Do you know what he has done for me, for me and Elaine? Has he told you?'

'About the job in Algiers? Yes. I'm—so glad for you both, if you are,' she said awkwardly, wishing she had warning of the terms they were supposed to be on, after his shocked reawakening to his need of Elaine and hers of him. *Did* infatuation die so suddenly? She hoped so.

Evidently as embarrassed as she, he muttered, 'I'm sorry, Tara. I've pestered you. I couldn't believe that you—— That you could *love* Dracon. That you could have fallen for him so soon after—me. You see, I thought our affair had a future, and I confess I almost forgot Elaine. And when you came here and Dracon flaunted you, and she was a kind of living reproach to my conscience, I began to take out my anger on both of you—and couldn't stop.

'And then Dracon kept on riding me down, and that —that *harpy*, Ninon, got hold of me and wormed out of me how we met and how you had jilted me for Dracon. Then you *married* him, and I suppose that should have brought me to my senses. But even if it had, there seemed to be no way back for me to Elaine until——'

'Until this afternoon, when you were afraid it might be too late to go back to her?' Tara suggested gently. 'But had you tried very hard until then?'

'Only in my mind. As far as she knew, I didn't even want to.'

'But you have talked to her now? You know why she took out Le Loup this afternoon?'

'Yes, she told me. And then—all right, I'm not ashamed to say so—we both cried all over each other, and I told her about Algiers, and then—well, we were back where we were before. Before—you happened.'

'And she doesn't know about me?'

'No.'

'And never will?'

'Never. I have hidden behind telling her I've behaved as I have because I was so frustrated in my job and fretting against Dracon's rule of law that choked me. Besides,' he smiled rather sheepishly, 'you won't like this, but I have a feeling that, even for me, you are going to look like a bit of wild-oat sowing that was experience at the time, but nothing more. Do you mind?'

Tara laughed aloud, and this time her head did not protest. 'Not a bit,' she assured him. 'Rather novel, really, to be noted in someone's mind as mere "experience". I must remember that for the future. It should stop me from getting a swelled head.'

'You've got one now. It is quite fat,' Charlot pointed out with a salty candour which cleared their way to ease with each other. Ease and no guilty looking back.

When he had left her Tara hugged to herself the two happinesses she had. Elaine's brief message—'Thank Tara for everything. She will understand.' And Dracon's parting shot which could mean anything or nothing, but which he had turned into promise with a smile in which the sun had risen for her. She had to be ready for him when he came ...

She was surprised to find she was quite hungry for the dinner which Mathilde brought her on a tray. She said so, and Mathilde explained, 'It is because you have had a weight lifted. You were desperately worried for Elaine, as we all were, but now you are enjoying the relief.'

'Yes, that must be it,' Tara agreed, having drunk her soup and now beginning on the delicate *goujons* of sole. But she knew it was more than relief. It was hope.

She begged Mathilde to go down to her own dinner, saying she was quite able to undress alone. Though she did not say so, she wanted to be alone, to make a leisurely task of it, to fill in time until Dracon came back.

While she was in her bathroom a maid came to re-make and turn down her bed. Tara refrained as far as possible from looking at her misshapen and blackening temple and brow. But Dracon had already seen them and hadn't seemed revolted. Why had he pretended to have waited to be asked to come to say goodnight to her? The Dracon *she* knew didn't look for permission. He came and went as he pleased.

On a fanciful whim she took from her wardrobe one of the satin nightgowns he had insisted she wear on their honeymoon. When he came, she would be in bed and covered up, but still—— She had just slipped it over her head and was taking sensual pleasure in smoothing it down, when he knocked and came in.

'Oh,' she said. 'You're early. I'm not in bed yet.'

'Obviously.'

But as she moved towards the bed he stopped her. 'No. Not there tonight,' he said.

She looked her blank surprise. 'Not here? Wh-why not?'

'Because it is your bed. I prefer ours.'

'Ours? But we haven't—— There isn't——'

'There is now. Simone and Belle, good souls, have done a *blitzkrieg* on the blue suite. The decorators only left this noon, but now it is—more or less—the *chambre de noces* which Mathilde was disappointed you couldn't occupy when I brought you back from Paris. But will you come now—with me?'

This must be a dream. She would wake up—— She heard herself murmur, 'Do you want me to?'

For reply he looked about him. 'Have you anything to put on? This?' He handed her the matching negligé which she had thrown across the foot of the bed. She put it on. Dracon took her hand and she went with him, the satin weaving and floating behind her as she walked.

The blue suite was on the first floor. In the process of the work on it, Tara and Elaine and Mathilde had watched the walls becoming a delicate bird's-egg blue; the hangings were a deep blue silk brocade; the huge bed was canopied in blue and silver; two dressing-rooms opened off.

Dracon left Tara to go to his, and she moved about the room, tracing with her finger the convoluted lines of the silver candlesticks on the dressing-table, admiring the silver-framed standing mirror, touching the silk of coverlet and curtains—just in case.

In case of what? Lest, after all, it shouldn't be her wedding apartment, her marriage bed . . .

Then Dracon was there, as he had been that night

in Paris—in his knee-length robe, his torso bare. He
said, 'There should have been champagne, but I hesitated to mix it with the sedatives you've had.' He sat
down on the bed. 'Come here.'

She went to him, letting the negligé slide from her
shoulders on the way. When she sat beside him, he
slipped to the floor, knelt, looking up at her, his hands
on her lap.

She longed to take his head between her hands, or
to wind her arms about his shoulders, drawing him to
her. But supposing this wasn't all it seemed? Supposing he had brought her here, only to reject her yet
again?

She found her voice. 'What did you mean when you
said you thought I would never ask?'

'Just that.'

'But why should my wanting you to wish me goodnight mean anything to you?'

'Little enough in itself.' He took one of her hands
and played with its fingers. 'But it was an opening, a
crack in the wall which would never have been
breached if you hadn't made it, leaving the widening to
me.'

'But do you want to widen it—in a wall that has
been of your making?' she asked shakily, not daring to
hope that at last he wanted of her what she wanted of
him—the physical things that were the ultimate expression of love, the shudder of expectant nerves, the
touch of flesh on flesh in a sweet, true, shared intimacy
she had yet to know with him.

'Of yours too,' he countered. 'You have done some walling up yourself, of all that you have kept from me. Meaning to tell me ever? Or never, who knows? But no matter now——' He stood and took her into his arms. 'Now I want you ... *want* you, and I'll get some response from you if it's the last thing I do. We've done with charades and force and outraged rejection. Now my body is going to speak to yours, and yours is going to answer—willingly, craving to—— We shouldn't need words.'

They did not, as he crushed her to him, his mouth seeking and parting her lips in a long kiss which was in itself a question demanding an answer. Tara gave it in the kisses she returned, in her little throaty murmurs of delight, in the restless movement of her hands, hungry to caress the texture, animal-warm and male, of his skin.

They touched, nuzzled and strained together, two primitive, sensate creatures, obeying their instinctive need to be one. Gently at last, Dracon pressed her down to the bed and was with her there, coaxing and gentling her towards ecstasy, and this time, though those four revealing words remained unspoken, she was not afraid. And when his body was hers for the taking, her own was ready to welcome it and cherish it and fulfil its utmost need.

There was a moment of exquisite pain, forgotten as it passed, then a throbbing urgency to take and to give, and at last a swelling tide of achievement which tossed them to a peak of consummated desire ... and ebbed, leaving them spent but transported, even tremulously laughing.

Dracon kissed her eyelids and her hair, walked his fingers in light play on her shoulders and down her arm. 'Delicious. Beyond my dreams. You would think we'd invented marriage, wouldn't you?' he asked.

She hid her face in the hollow of his shoulder. Her voice came muffled as she said, 'I thought I should have to tell you, but tonight I think you knew, didn't you?'

'Knew what, my heart?'

She lifted her head. 'You *did*!' she accused. 'Not that night in Paris. That night I had steeled myself to say "I'm a virgin", and let you make what you could of that and of my willingness to let you conclude, and to go on thinking otherwise, of me. In Paris, you couldn't have known. But tonight you did. How?'

'What makes you think I didn't know in Paris? Though I was puzzled, since there had been Charlot and you had never denied your profession, I think I guessed, when I made very gentle love to you and you cried. You were frightened, as no experienced girl would have been——'

'I was beginning to be ill.'

'But your rejection of me was something different. Though when I accepted it and left you, do you remember what I said?'

Memory flashed light. 'Ye-s, now. You said you'd been left with damp squibs on the Fourteenth of July!'

'Trying to tell you what?'

'I didn't know. I was "away out of my head", as they say in Ireland. But—you were disappointed in me?'

'Not in you, lovely one. In a marriage on which I had counted to clear up everything between us. Because I had used what I had told you was necessity for Elaine's sake, to get you, to possess you for my own. Forgive me for that, can you?'

Tara laughed. 'If you can forgive me for saying Yes to you because I wanted to *be* possessed, and not only because—as I tried to tell myself—that I should be saving you from Ninon Chauvet! But even when you had guessed that you were the first man for me, you never asked me about it, nor came near me for love again. Why not?'

'It wasn't guesswork for long. I told Doctor Matisse that you had talked nonsense while you were delirious, but you had said quite distinctly, "Please, Dracon, I am still a virgin. Try to understand." And though I should have pitied you, that hardened me against you. You could have trusted me on our wedding night. But you hadn't. From the beginning you could have put me right about your not being the call-girl I thought you. But you hadn't——'

'Don't tell me you'd begun to guess that too!'

'Begun? After one tantalising hour in your company I had suspected it. You were too proud, too aware of insult to be the *demi-mondaine* I'd expected had bewitched Charlot. But, virtuous or not, you *had* helped him to waste his time—*my* time, and you had, on your own admission, meant to encourage him again when you came here.'

'Not after I knew the truth about Elaine! And so'—Tara was working it out—'for all this you had to punish me by never missing a trick in taunting me and treating me as the tramp you already guessed I wasn't. That was—cruel.'

Dracon did not answer at once. Then, 'The cruelty was for myself, to cure myself of you if you weren't, after all, everything I hoped you were. The rest was designed to force you to break and defend yourself against me, which I thought you must do in time. But I'd reckoned without that proud spirit of yours, my darling. You didn't break. And I wasn't cured.'

'Are you sure?' she taunted gently, forgiving him.

'Would you rather I weren't?' he teased back. 'Would you rather that I kept you here as my light-o'-love for an hour, and then packed you back to your own room for another aching aeon of separation and huff?'

She giggled in happy abandonment. 'Just try!' she dared him.

'I am trying.'

But he wasn't. He was touching her breasts, tracing the long line of her thigh, arousing her to new desires which he meant to satisfy again.

Later he said, 'You "asked" only just in time. When I thought I might have lost you this afternoon, if only you were spared to me, I meant to take you tonight—or else!'

Tara raised heavy, sated eyes to his. 'So I hoped,' she told him. 'You called me by some lovely names while you thought I was unconscious. *That* was why I asked.'

Much later still, after they had slept in each other's arms, Dracon said broodingly, 'I am still Leloupblanc and I have to lead my pack. That you are going to have to face.'

Less awake than he, Tara murmured, 'Yes, so they warned me. You are arrogant and masterful and dictatorial and always—you. But lead away, my wolf, and I'll try——' she stifled a luxurious yawn—'I'll try to follow.'

What readers say about Harlequin Romances

"Harlequins take away the world's troubles and for a while you can live in a world of your own where love reigns supreme."
L.S.,* Beltsville, Maryland

"Thank you for bringing romance back to me."
J.W., Tehachapi, California

"I find Harlequins are the only stories on the market that give me a satisfying romance with sufficient depth without being maudlin."
C.S., Bangor, Maine

"Harlequins are magic carpets...away from pain and depression...away to other people and other countries one might never know otherwise."
H.R., Akron, Ohio

*Names available on request

Harlequin Romances

The books that let you escape
into the wonderful world of romance!
Trips to exotic places…interesting
plots…meeting memorable people…
the excitement of love…. These are
integral parts of Harlequin Romances –
the heartwarming novels read by
women everywhere.

Many early issues are now available.
Choose from this great selection!

Choose from this list of Harlequin Romance editions.*

Some of these book were originally published under different titles.

Relive a great love story…
with Harlequin Romances
Complete and mail this coupon today!

Harlequin Reader Service

In U.S.A.
MPO Box 707
Niagara Falls, N.Y. 14302

In Canada
649 Ontario St.
Stratford, Ontario, N5A 6W2

Please send me the following Harlequin Romance novels. I am enclosing my check or money order for $1.25 for each novel ordered, plus 59¢ to cover postage and handling.

☐ 422	☐ 509	☐ 636	☐ 729	☐ 810	☐ 902
☐ 434	☐ 517	☐ 673	☐ 737	☐ 815	☐ 903
☐ 459	☐ 535	☐ 683	☐ 746	☐ 838	☐ 909
☐ 481	☐ 559	☐ 684	☐ 748	☐ 872	☐ 920
☐ 492	☐ 583	☐ 713	☐ 798	☐ 878	☐ 927
☐ 508	☐ 634	☐ 714	☐ 799	☐ 888	☐ 941

Number of novels checked @ $1.25 each = $_____

N.Y. and Ariz. residents add appropriate sales tax. $_____

Postage and handling $_____ .59

TOTAL $_____

I enclose _____
(Please send check or money order. We cannot be responsible for cash sent through the mail.)

Prices subject to change without notice.

NAME _____
(Please Print)

ADDRESS _____

CITY _____

STATE/PROV. _____

ZIP/POSTAL CODE _____

Offer expires September 30, 1981.   104564271